A CHRISTMAS WITH THE FROSTY LORD

CHRISTMAS REGENCY ROMANCE

CHARLOTTE DARCY PALMER

FAIR HAVENS BOOKS

REGENCY CHRISTMAS.

.

The Christmas season was a little more defined in the Regency era than it is nowadays. I thought you might like to know a few of the Regency traditions.

The season would officially start with **Stir it up Sunday**. This took place on the fourth Sunday before Christmas – the beginning of Advent.

The family would gather to make Christmas puddings. These needed to age before serving and would arrive at the Christmas dinner served flaming.

Many people believe it was called Stir it up Sunday because of the stirring of the puddings, however, it was after the main prayer in the Book of Common Prayer for that day, "Stir up, we beseech thee, O Lord, the wills of thy faithful people; that they, plenteously bringing forth the fruit of good works, may of thee be plenteously rewarded; through Jesus Christ our Lord. Amen."

Christmastide visiting would begin on St Nicholas Day –

December 6th. Often small gifts were exchanged between children on this day.

Thomasing was allowed on December 21st then being St Thomas's Day. (St Thomas Day has since been moved to July 3rd.)

It was a custom in rural England where the poor and especially elderly widowed women could go door to door asking for handouts so that they may have something good to eat at Christmas.

There is an old song about the custom:

Christmas is coming and the geese are getting fat.

Please spare a penny for the old man's hat.

If you haven't got a penny, a ha'penny will do.

If you haven't got a ha'penny, God bless you.

Christmas Eve

Houses would be decorated with greenery, such as holly and ivy, hawthorn, bay, laurel, rosemary, and the Christmas rose Hellebore.

Some would fashion kissing boughs from mistletoe with added ribbons and apples.

These decorations stayed in place until Epiphany when they were taken down and were actually burned to prevent bad luck.

Christmas Day

Would begin with a visit to church. Gift giving was not as traditional as it is today. Children may receive small gifts as may the romantically inclined. Servants would often receive a gift at the Christmas dinner.

The Christmas dinner was a magnificent feast. Roast goose or a boars head would be the main meat. Brawn, a potted meat dish would often be served. Minced meat pies were also a favorite and could be called Christmas or Twelfth Night pies. These eventually evolved into the fruited mince pies of today but in this era were a meat product.

Left-over meat from the meal would be used to make more pies for the twelve days until Epiphany. It was a custom that eating a minced pie each of the twelve days of Christmas would bring twelve months of happiness for the New Year.

The meal would be rounded off with the pudding made of stir it up Sunday. A sprig of Holly would be placed on top of the pudding as a reminder of Jesus' Crown of Thorns.

The pudding would be doused with brandy and set aflame as a centerpiece of the meal.

December 26th Boxing Day or St Stephen's Day

Giving Christmas Boxes to charity and servants was a custom on St Stephen's day which became Boxing Day. Old clothing and other items would be handed to the servants who might also get the day off.

This was also a traditional day for hunting and for theaters to open their Christmas Pantomimes.

New Year's Eve – December 31st

Not all traditions were practiced by all the country but here are a few:

Some gathered their family and friends into a circle before midnight. At the stroke of the hour the head of the family would usher out the old by opening the door and then he would welcome in the new.

First Footer

This was a more Northern England and Scottish tradition – the first foot to cross the threshold after the New Year would affect the family's fortunes for the year to come.

The best first footer would be a tall, dark, handsome male especially if his feet had high insteps. This implied that water – or bad luck would flow right through them.

Women or flat-footed men were usually but not always bad omens. In some instances bare-footed blonde or redheaded girls could bring good luck.

New Year's Day January 1ˢᵗ

Was considered a day that could predict the fortunes of the year. One tradition was to hook a flat cake on to the horns of a cow. If it fell off the front, it foretold good luck. If it fell behind the cow it foretold bad luck.

Creaming the Well

Young women would race to draw the first water. Possession of this water meant marriage that year.

Burning the Bush

In Hertfordshire a hawthorn bush would be burned on New Year's Day to bring good luck and a bountiful harvest.

Twelfth Night – January 6ᵗʰ

The Twelfth Night or Epiphany was the climax of Christmastide. It was a feast and the traditional time to exchange gifts.

Decorations would be taken down and burned by midnight on this day to prevent bad luck for the year.

Masks and balls were very popular on this day. Twelfth-day cakes would be made in elaborate designs. These were expensive for the time and covered in colored sugar. The night would be full of games and dancing and most likely rowdy celebrations. Twelfth night gained such a bad reputation that in the 1870's Queen Victoria outlawed its celebration for fear that the celebrations were out of control.

I also have a three book Christmas Regency Box Set currently just 0.99 and FREE on KU Get The Duke, The Earl & The Joker now.

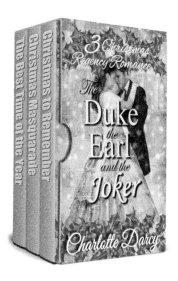

Get a FREE eBook The Shallow Waters of Romance and find out about Charlotte's new releases by joining her newsletter here.

CHAPTER 1

"My dear Rosalind, how very nice you look this evening." Wentworth Blackwood, the Duke of Newfield, was as warm and as complimentary as ever.

Rosalind could not help but wonder if he would utter the very same words if she had turned up to the Duke's winter ball in her riding outfit, and an old, worn cloak. She somehow thought he would.

"You flatter me, Your Grace." Rosalind smiled at his pleasant face.

The Duke was portly, with an almost full head of grey hair and a ruddy complexion. His pale blue eyes shone under the light of the chandeliers and they looked upon her in a kindly way, as was his custom.

"I think a bright young lady such as yourself should always be flattered." The Duke countered with a beaming smile.

"Papa, you will make Rosalind embarrassed." Lady Claudette

Blackwood, the Duke's daughter, shook her head a little and laughed.

"I am always being chastised by my daughter." The Duke continued amiably. "What about you, Leighton? Does dear Rosalind here snap at your heels like a hunting dog or boss you around like the fiercest governess?" The Duke clapped a hand on the Earl of Leighton's back.

"Oh, yes. Especially as yuletide draws nearer, it must be said." Rosalind's father laughed and nodded.

"And why do you find yourself more harshly treated at Yuletide?" The Duke was warming to his theme and enjoying it immensely.

Rosalind was enjoying herself very much also. She liked the warm atmosphere at Newfield Hall and had lately found that she had a good deal in common with Claudette, the Duke's daughter. She felt sure that their friendship would continue to grow and that she would, undoubtedly, become a more regular visitor to Newfield Hall on account of it.

"Because that is when Rosalind begins making all her plans for the Christmas celebrations at Leighton Hall. It all seems to begin in November, and so I do what I can to keep out of the way." He laughed.

"Papa!"

"But I must admit, it is always worth it. Rosalind always makes Christmas at Leighton Hall very special indeed. She always finds something a little bit different for us all to do."

"Indeed, she does, I remember well last year's theatrical. Very good, very clever." The Duke turned to Rosalind and smiled.

"Thank you, Your Grace," Rosalind said graciously. "And I must admit, I enjoy it more than anything."

"You do not find so many preparations tiring, Rosalind?" Claudette was studying Rosalind intently. "I mean, it does seem like an awful lot of hard work to lay on a Christmas that is so very full of things to do?"

"It is rather a lot of hard work, but it is something that always excites me. I find that come October I am already thinking of Christmas. It is a most wonderful celebration for everybody, is it not? It is a time for friends and family, and a time to show the staff how much you appreciate their efforts throughout the year. Not to mention a little charity along the way. It is a most charitable time, is it not?"

"Yes, it is. But to manage it all, one must be so very organized," Claudette said with a comical grimace.

"I suppose so, but the skills of organization can very quickly be learned."

"Well, that is settled then," The Duke said, and everybody turned to look at him quizzically.

"What is settled, Papa?" Claudette asked dubiously.

"Claudette, you must arrange Christmas here at Newfield Hall. You must make it exciting and packed with wonderful things to do, just as Rosalind does at Leighton Hall. What do you say?" He had sidled around to his daughter who looked as if she were making ready to run.

"But, Papa."

"My dear girl, you need not look as if you had been cornered in the whole thing."

"But I have, Papa. You have cornered me completely."

3

Claudette laughed, but Rosalind could sense the consternation beneath it all.

"But it would be fun, would it not? It would certainly keep you occupied from now until twelfth night." He shrugged as if he truly were doing her a great favor.

"Well, what sort of things would you like me to arrange, Papa?" Claudette's pretty face was wrinkled in a frown.

"That would be up to you, my dear. You are to have a free hand in all of it. There, am I not a generous father?"

"I do not know how to answer that, Papa, really I do not," Claudette said, and the entire party laughed.

"You never know, Claudette, you might come to enjoy it. I know that it keeps our dear Rosalind happily occupied." Rosalind's mother, Lady Beatrice, was clearly trying to soothe the young woman's nerves.

"Lady Beatrice, I am not as organized as Rosalind." Claudette turned to look at Rosalind for confirmation.

"Claudette, you must not worry about it," Rosalind said gently. "And I will help you, I promise."

"You really will help me?" Claudette looked like a drowning woman who had been thrown a rope.

"Of course, I shall. I shall help you with every bit of it."

"Dear me, what does Claudette need help with?" Suddenly, Gabriel Blackwood, the Duke's son, appeared at Rosalind's side.

He appeared so suddenly that she almost gasped, but hurriedly steadied herself and turned a little to look up at him. Gabriel was very tall, taller even than his father, and standing next to him made Rosalind feel like a child.

"With the Christmas festivities, Gabriel." It was clear that Claudette had gathered herself a good deal following Rosalind's offer of assistance.

"Oh dear, are we to have Christmas festivities?" Gabriel's tone was flat and, Rosalind thought, just a little sarcastic for her taste.

"Of course, we are, Gabriel. You have not been gone so long that you forget that we celebrate Christmas, have you?" His father laughed but Rosalind thought she detected a little annoyance in his tone.

"Yes, I remember, Father. But I must admit, I remember it being something of a quiet affair." Although his tone was still flat, the sarcasm had very wisely been dispensed with.

"Well, it is time to change all that," The Duke said, also regaining his former jollity.

Rosalind wondered at the cause of the little tension between the two men, and she wondered if anybody else had noticed it. Gabriel had not seemed to enjoy the winter ball his father had thrown at all, and had spent all evening keeping himself in quiet conversation here and there about the large ballroom, and very determinedly avoiding the dancing.

"Yes, we are going to have a much jollier Christmas this year, brother," Claudette said with a bright smile. "And I am going to arrange it. Well, with Rosalind's help, at any rate."

"But Lady Rosalind will be busy with her own family celebrations, will she not?" He turned to look directly at her, as if the question he had asked his sister demanded an answer from Rosalind herself.

Something about his attitude annoyed her greatly and she wished that he had not come over to join the little party in the first place.

After all, Rosalind had hardly insisted that the Duke of Newfield celebrate Christmas in any particular way at all. She had simply offered to help when he had cast the responsibility for it all at his daughter.

"I am very well used to organizing Christmas events, Lord Gabriel," she said, choosing to be as formal in her address as he had been. "So, I will certainly have time on my hands to help Claudette, if she needs my help, that is."

"Oh, yes, I shall need your help," Claudette said, clearly wanting to emphasize her need for assistance.

"Then it is settled." Rosalind turned away from Gabriel and smiled at Claudette. "Perhaps we should arrange an afternoon tea this week, my dear, so that we might discuss the whole thing?" She had become suddenly determined to let the son of the Duke know that she would not be cowed by his disdain.

"Oh, yes, please, I would be most grateful."

"And you really will be a tremendous success, Claudette, I have no doubt at all."

"Oh, that is kind, Rosalind," Claudette said, and Gabriel was forced to stand aside a little as his sister made her way to Rosalind and quickly grasped her hand. "You have given me confidence that the whole thing will go very well."

"My dear Lady Rosalind, I think you might find yourself very busy over the next few weeks." Gabriel laughed. "Because it certainly looks as if you now have the responsibility for arranging Christmas for two households."

"I am only arranging one, sir." Rosalind fought to keep her tone light. "And I will simply be providing a little assistance in the arrangement of the other."

"If you say so."

"I must say, Rosalind, I think I am beginning to look forward to it all." Claudette spoke brightly, a little too brightly, and it was clear to Rosalind that she sought to compensate for her brother's mean-spirited conversation.

"And I am looking forward to it too, Claudette. We will manage the thing very well indeed and it will be a Christmas to remember for us all."

CHAPTER 2

"How ow good of you to come out to tea so soon. You have had only one day's rest after the ball, my dear Rosalind." Claudette hurried her into a seat in the immense drawing room of Newfield Hall.

As Rosalind perched daintily on a soft, pale green velvet covered couch, she thought that her father's drawing room at Leighton Hall would easily fit inside the one at Newfield four times over.

"I am perfectly well rested, Claudette, and have been looking forward to getting on with things," Rosalind said warmly. "Now tell me, are you over the shock of your father handing you so great a responsibility, and so *suddenly*?"

"Not really," Claudette said and both women laughed. "He does get so excited, so carried away with things. It is just like him to hear about your Christmases and decide, on a whim, we must do the same. But he is such a wonderful father, so kind and so amusing, that I would not wish to let him down in any way."

"I cannot think for a minute that you are going to let him down, my dear. I am here to help you at every step."

"And I am very grateful." Claudette settled herself down on the opposite couch. "I have already sent for some tea, it should not be too long."

"Well, in the meantime, we could discuss a few of the little ideas that I have had for you," Rosalind said and felt suddenly purposeful. "In fact, I have come up with a list of things, little events that you might care to try out, if you would like." Rosalind began to rummage through her velvet drawstring purse.

Just as she was pulling a sheet of paper from the purse, the door to the drawing room opened abruptly. Both women looked up, Rosalind fully expecting to see a footman with a tea tray, only to see Gabriel Blackwood staring back at them.

"Forgive me, I had not realized you had company, sister," he said in that same flat tone.

"Good afternoon, Lord Gabriel," Rosalind said with a watery smile.

"Good afternoon, Lady Rosalind." He nodded politely, as if remembering his manners. "I trust you are well?"

"I am very well, sir, I thank you." She inclined her head graciously, and wished that he would go away.

"Tea should be with us at any moment, Gabriel, if you would care to join us?" Claudette seemed hopeful and Rosalind could not help but wonder why.

After all, if Gabriel was her own brother, Rosalind would not seek to include him at all. She would simply let him stew in whatever ill humor it was that had overtaken him until he decided for himself to climb out of it.

"Well, I would not wish to intrude." He began and there was just the slightest softening of his tone.

"You would not be intruding at all, Gabriel," Claudette said warmly. "We are only discussing plans for Christmas."

"Then I will leave you two ladies to your plotting and scheming." He nodded again with the faintest flicker of a smile.

Rosalind noted that a smile improved his looks greatly. He was certainly a very handsome young man; of that there was no doubt, but his current surly aspect seemed to detract from it greatly.

Gabriel was tall and broadly built, with the dark hair that his father once had, and the unmistakable pale blue eyes.

He had the sort of dark skin that looked ready to sprout a full beard at any moment if he did not keep his mind on it, and very strong features. He had a good chin and a straight nose, and was very likely already the talk of many a drawing room now that he had returned from Europe.

Rosalind had no doubt that there were excited mothers the length and breadth of the county all wondering how best to throw their own daughters in the path of the young man who would one day be the Duke of Newfield.

"As you wish, Gabriel." Claudette smiled sweetly.

Without another word, Gabriel simply gave them a curt nod before retreating and closing the door behind him. For a moment, Claudette remained silent and Rosalind knew that she was struggling in some way. She had no doubt that

Claudette was a little embarrassed about her brother's somewhat abrupt manner, but it seemed as if she was sad also, upset somehow.

"You really must forgive my brother, Rosalind." Claudette began quietly. "I think he is having a little trouble settling back into life in England again."

"You need not apologize at all, my dear. Your brother is perfectly pleasant." Rosalind said with such warmth that she almost believed it herself.

The truth was that Gabriel Blackwood was far from pleasant. He was certainly not the young man that she remembered prior to his grand tour of Europe.

As did so many fine young men of the age, Gabriel had spent three years touring Europe with his tutor, learning a little something about the world. It was a journey that was looked upon as a means of a young man rounding off his education, becoming cultured even. It was an experience designed to add knowledge and polish to a young man of already good breeding.

However, whilst she did not doubt he had gained knowledge, Rosalind could not begin to imagine that he had returned *polished*.

"That is so sweet of you, Rosalind, but he is not particularly pleasant. If I am honest, I can hardly recognize him as my brother anymore. He seems so dissatisfied with home now that he has returned."

"But did he not wish to return?" Rosalind said, knowing that she was perhaps prying a little.

"No, he did not wish to return." Claudette spoke quietly, almost as if Gabriel himself was still in the room. "I think he had wanted to stay away for the full four years, but Papa had only ever really wanted him to be in Europe for two. In the end, Gabriel's grand tour lasted three years before my father demanded his return."

"And Gabriel resents it?"

"Yes, I think he does. But my father already gave him such leeway. And I think he is lucky to have gone at all, for any little trip to Europe I can expect will last no more than a few weeks, and that I know well." Claudette sighed. "Forgive me, I did not mean to sound bitter."

"You do not sound bitter, my dear," Rosalind said genuinely. "And you are right, I do not think that there are many young men who realize quite what privileges they have in life. Everything is at their feet, and they have access to as much learning and sightseeing as they care to have. Perhaps that is part of the problem. When a person sees something as their right, they perhaps do not appreciate it as much as somebody who does not have that same sense of entitlement. The value becomes greater the more you have to work for it.""

"That is exactly the truth, Rosalind. You and I would certainly have appreciated the whole experience, I am sure." Claudette seemed relieved to have somebody understand her. "But I love my brother dearly, and I just wish that he was the same young man today as the young man who left three years ago. But he has changed. He has become cynical, almost sneering at times. It is as if he is dissatisfied with everything around him, and everyone. There is an impatience about him and an air, at times, of simply tolerating my father and me."

"Perhaps it is simply because he has been away for so long," Rosalind said, wondering how it was that a young man could change so much. "And if that is the case, all that is needed to put the thing right is simply time."

"I do hope that you are right, Rosalind, for your words do give me such comfort. You give me hope that things really might improve. I have been so worried, you see, that Europe has changed him so much that he will never be satisfied to be here with us again. Perhaps he thinks he has become a little too cultured for us."

"And perhaps he will quickly learn that he has not," Rosalind said, and felt a stab of annoyance at Gabriel Blackwood for causing his sister such pain. "Because it does not matter where you go in this world, does it? I mean, wherever you go, *there you are*. You are always yourself beneath it all, whatever influences might be all around you. But with those influences becoming a distant memory, I am sure that your brother will return to himself again. He just needs time of his own to settle in, I am sure of it."

"Rosalind, you really have made me feel so much better. You are very wise, my dear," Claudette said and smiled sweetly.

At that moment, Rosalind felt something of a fraud. After all, she had simply sought to make Claudette feel better. Whether or not Gabriel Blackwood really would return to himself, Rosalind truly had no idea.

"Well, let me read you my little list of ideas. That might cheer you up, Claudette." Rosalind gave her a broad smile, hoping that Christmas, at least, might help to bring that family back together again.

CHAPTER 3

*B*eing just a party of six, it was possible for them all to travel in the Duke's carriage. Rosalind was pleased that her mother and father, the Earl and Countess of Leighton, seemed to be throwing themselves into things, full of Christmas cheer.

And, as for the Duke himself, and Claudette, they were both rosy cheeked with excitement about the curious little Christmas event that Rosalind had suggested for them all.

In truth, it had not taken a good deal of arranging. They had only one festive song to sing, one which they were all already quite familiar with, so there had been little effort in that.

And when Rosalind had suggested that they travel the area one evening together and stop at several of their closest neighbors' homes to sing them a song and share a drink with them, wishing them a joyous yuletide, it had been met with excitement all around. Except for Gabriel Blackwood, of course.

Gabriel had not practiced with the two families on the three occasions they had met for just such a purpose. He had claimed to be familiar enough with the song *Here We Come A-Wassailing*, that he need not involve himself with such preparations.

"This really is a very good idea of yours, Rosalind." The Duke said loudly as the carriage rumbled along. "But I hope that we do not catch our neighbors so unaware that they will not even have time to prepare a warm drink for us."

"You need have no fear of that, Your Grace," Rosalind said happily. "For Claudette has written to everybody individually to let them know of our little plan. So, you see, we will be expected, and therefore treated very well."

"I wonder if our neighbors really *will* be so very pleased to have us singing on their doorsteps," Gabriel said sullenly.

"I think it is a wonderful old custom, Gabriel," Lady Beatrice said in a motherly tone.

"Yes, I am just not sure it is a custom that ought to be revived, Lady Beatrice."

"But it is being revived quite successfully all over the place, Lord Gabriel." The formality of address had continued to exist between the two of them. "And many people are taking part these days."

"I had no idea. Perhaps I really have been in Europe too long."

"Dear me, does nobody in Europe have any fun at all?" Rosalind said waspishly and was relieved when the Duke himself boomed with laughter.

"Yes, they do, Lady Rosalind." Gabriel was clearly not

amused. "But perhaps they amuse themselves with less *simplicity*."

Rosalind smiled and shrugged prettily, successfully hiding her offense. It was becoming clear to her that Claudette was right and Gabriel really did think himself too cultured now that he was returned to England. But she was determined not to let that spoil her own good fun. Yes, spending a frosty evening traveling from house to house singing for one's neighbors and wishing them the very best for the season was simple indeed. But perhaps that was its own brilliance, its simplicity.

"And perhaps simplicity is at the very heart of the Christmas spirit, Lord Gabriel."

"Let us hope that our neighbors think so."

The Duke immediately began to talk excitedly, clearly determined to squash the negative effect that his son was having on the entire party. And, being such a determinedly cheerful man, Wentworth Blackwood soon had almost everybody in the carriage laughing and chattering excitedly about the evening to come.

The first home they were to visit was that of Mr. Bartholomew Altman and his wife and daughters. They were a fine old family who had lived in the county for generations and were very good friends to both the Duke and the Earl.

"We are here! We have arrived!" Claudette said with barely contained excitement when the carriage finally drew to a halt. "Really, I can hardly believe how excited I am."

"As am I, my dear." Rosalind squeezed her friend's hand.

Rosalind was pleased to note the excitement of them all, barring Gabriel, as they climbed down from the carriage on a wave of happy chatter. There was much clearing of throats and practicing of the first line as they made their way to the front door of the Altman house.

"Right, is everybody ready?" Rosalind asked, as she busily arranged to them neatly around the door. "Now, perhaps as the tallest, you might stand next to your father at the back, Lord Gabriel," Rosalind said and gently pushed Gabriel towards his father. She then went on to arrange her own family and Claudette until they looked like a very neat, professional outfit.

"I say, do we knock on the door, or do we simply start singing?" The Duke said loudly.

Fighting an urge to laugh at the idea that his booming voice was indication enough to all inside that the party had arrived, Rosalind made a pretense of giving the matter some thought.

"Perhaps we ought to just start singing," she said airily. "I suppose this being our first one, we will be able to flatten out any problems that might arise. This can be our practice, can it not?"

"Right, well, I am ready when you are." The Duke said and cleared his throat loudly for the fourth time.

"I hope everybody is ready to sing heartily," Rosalind said and looked directly at Gabriel.

"Yes, if I can remember the words," Gabriel said quietly, as everybody else murmured their agreement.

"Here," Rosalind said, handing him a sheet of paper that she had drawn from the pocket of her cloak. "I had a feeling that you might make this particular objection." She had to stand on tiptoe to whisper her annoyance into his ear. "So now there is no excuse, is there?" She pushed the piece of paper into his hand with the words for the song neatly written upon it.

Rosalind quickly made her way to the front of the little group and counted down to the opening line of the song, just as they had rehearsed it. As soon as they began to sing, she joined in, turning to face the door and wait for Mr. Altman to open it.

"Here we come a-wassailing

Among the leaves so green.

Here we come a-wand'ring

So fair to be seen."

The little group sang so beautifully that Rosalind could hardly believe it. They had done well in their practices, but there seemed to be something so very magical about the reality of it all that it had boosted their voices, making them richer and stronger.

When Mr. Altman opened the door, it was clear that he, his wife, and their daughters, were more than ready for them. They were all neatly dressed, as if ready for dinner, and fully expecting guests. And their pleasure as the song continued was very obvious. Everything was working out so well and Rosalind was enjoying herself so much that she had all but forgotten Gabriel's resistance, not to mention her own obvious annoyance at him.

When the song reached its conclusion, the Altman's clapped loudly, Mr Altman standing back to allow them all admittance.

"How lovely that was," Mrs. Altman said as she ushered them

all into the drawing room where there was already a roaring fire and a tray full of cups of hot, spiced wine. "Such a wonderful idea."

"This is just the beginning of things, Mrs. Altman," Claudette said, her eyes shining with a mixture of excitement and relief that the thing had gone well. "For Lady Rosalind and I have been planning all sorts of other wonderful Christmas events that we dearly hope you will be able to attend."

"If you have planned the rest with such gusto, my dear Lady Claudette, you may be assured of my family's attendance," Mr. Altman said as they all fell into a wonderfully relaxed conversation, drinking their hot wine by the fireside.

"Well, if nothing else, you have made my sister happy," Gabriel said, although his tone was less sardonic.

"Tell me, do you always choose your words so purposefully, Lord Gabriel?" Rosalind gave him an angry look. *"If nothing else?"* She shook her head and kept her voice low, keen that the little crowd in happy conversation about the fireplace should not hear them. "The only person who has not enjoyed themselves this evening, Lord Gabriel, is you. And the only reason that you have not enjoyed yourself, I have no doubt, is because you had already determined that you would not."

"You look at me with such an angry face," Gabriel said, and actually laughed. "You look quite fierce, my dear."

"I *am* quite fierce, Lord Gabriel," Rosalind growled in a tone which sought to warn him.

"Then I shall have to take care, shall I not?" He smiled at her suddenly, and she was struck by the transformation.

His pale blue eyes seemed to reflect the firelight and his smile made him look younger, more carefree. Still, Rosalind was determined not to fall into easy forgiveness just because he had a handsome face.

"We have a good deal more events to get through before Christmas is over and yes, Lord Gabriel, you really *will* have to take care." Rosalind warned, before smiling and turning away from him, to join the party around the fireplace.

CHAPTER 4

*I*n the week before Christmas Eve, Rosalind had been determined to gather up all her greenery for the many decorations she would have to make. She enjoyed making festive wreaths and garlands, it was true, but now that she had both Leighton Hall and Newfield Hall to think about, she would certainly have to work quickly.

Claudette was extremely excited by the prospect of learning how to make decorations with holly and other evergreens, but being new to it all, she would not yet be able to work quickly, Rosalind was sure.

"What on earth are you doing in here?" Gabriel had come upon her so suddenly that she almost jumped out of her skin.

"I am collecting greenery for the Christmas decorations, Lord Gabriel," she said in an agitated manner; Rosalind was annoyed with being startled for no reason. "And since the holly on your estate has berries this year, whereas the holly on my father's estate does not, the Duke said that I might come into your woodland and help myself." He was staring at her quizzically and, although he did not seem to be quite as disdainful as usual, his very presence still annoyed her. "I am not poaching, if that is what you are worried about. So, there will be no need to shout for the gamekeeper to come and take a shot at me."

"Good heavens, but you are hostile this morning, Lady Rosalind!" he said and threw his head back to laugh.

"Am I, indeed?" she said a little sullenly, annoyed with herself for allowing his sudden presence to unsettle her.

"Yes, peculiarly hostile," he was still smiling and she could not help but think he was taunting her a little.

"And is it any wonder?" Rosalind said, deciding to fight back.

"You are annoyed with me, I think."

"I daresay we are not well enough acquainted to be able to argue successfully, but I must defend myself."

"Absolutely," he said with an amused grin.

"I cannot quite work out your curious attitudes, Lord Gabriel."

"Then perhaps you can simply forgive them." He raised his eyebrows hopefully, but there was still something gently mocking in his countenance.

"To forgive without understanding? No, I do not think so."

"Then I shall persist no further," he said with a deep bow. "Since the lady would seem to be so hard-hearted."

"I am not hard-hearted, Lord Gabriel, but my patience has its limits."

"You really are a most extraordinary young woman, are you not?"

"Perhaps," she said neutrally, not sure whether his comment was a compliment or otherwise.

"Which is not meant as an insult." He smiled and shrugged.

"Perhaps you ought to wonder a little why it is you find yourself in a position of having to clarify such a thing. I think my confusion is very natural given your decidedly cold attitude at times."

"Yes, perhaps one ought to wonder at it," he said in a noncommittal fashion.

"Well, I should get on." She brandished her little scissors and reached out for a high, berry-laden holly branch.

"Allow me," he said, and pulled the branch down towards her so that she might easily reach to cut it.

"Are you collecting all of the greenery for both houses?" he asked, making an attempt at conversation.

"Yes, I am." She tried to lighten her tone considerably, given the uncomfortable turn that the conversation had taken.

"But why is Claudette not here to help?"

"Because she is a little unwell today. I am surprised that you did not know that already."

"I have not seen my sister this morning, but then I had breakfast before the rest of the family. I have not seen any of them."

"I see." Rosalind stopped herself from pointing out, *that* was most peculiar behavior.

"But why do you not have a servant with you? That would be easier, would it not?"

"Because I am personally able to gather ivy, holly, and mistletoe myself. And I enjoy it, Lord Gabriel."

"Please, just Gabriel."

"Ah, you have chosen to dispense with the formality. Since it was you, I remember, who seemed to insist upon it in the first place."

"You are quite determined for an argument this morning, are you not?" He laughed as he reached up to pull down another branch for her.

"No, I would not say that." Rosalind objected, even though she knew that he had spoken the truth.

There was something about Gabriel which made her not want to forgive him, even in that gentle way that a simple conversation would seem to forgive. She wanted him to know that she was annoyed with him, she even wanted him to apologize.

But there was something else too. There was something curiously attractive about him and Rosalind, aggravated by his character, was determined not to feel it.

"So, what are you making with your holly, ivy, and mistletoe?" He carried on regardless.

"Garlands with the holly and ivy," she said a little distractedly as she snipped another branch. "And I thought I would make a kissing bough for each house with ivy, mistletoe, and some rosemary. And ribbons and other such little adornments, of course."

"A kissing bough?" he said and raised his eyebrows.

"Is that really so very shocking?" Rosalind laughed.

"No, it is not shocking at all," he said sarcastically. "Really, I have traveled through Paris, Rome, the Netherlands, Venice, to name but a few. Do you really think I could be shocked by something so simple? By something so dreadfully innocent?"

"You are very determined to set yourself against the celebrations, are you not?" She paused for a moment and forced herself to look into his pale blue eyes. "No, forgive me... that is not quite right," she said, and enjoyed the build-up to a tidy little insult of her own. "I do not think you wish to set yourself *against* the celebrations, rather you wish to set yourself *above* them. And not just the celebrations, but everything and everyone around you." Once the words had left her lips, Rosalind wondered how much she would, or could regret them later.

"And that is what you think, is it?" he said, his frown apparent, and his countenance darkening into annoyance.

"What I think, sir, is that it is a wonderful thing to travel Europe and broaden one's horizons. I should love the opportunity to do something similar myself, although I am bound to say *that* will never happen." Rosalind wanted to remind him of the great privilege he had just enjoyed. "But if all one learns on such a grand tour is how to be cynical, then perhaps I ought to be glad that I do not have the opportunity in the first place."

"You think me cynical?" he asked in a most serious tone.

"Oh, I am sure of it."

"And does one have to be cynical not to throw oneself into the festive season? Is that all it takes?"

"No, it takes much more than that," she said, but determined not to point out any other of his flaws.

She thought she had gone quite far enough without suggesting that it was not only Christmas, but his own friends and family, which he had chosen to disdain.

"And I suppose you yourself are the very *spirit* of Christmas, Rosalind?"

"I am not the spirit of Christmas, Gabriel, but I do, at least, understand what that means." Rosalind was furious.

"Really? Are you absolutely sure this is all about the spirit of Christmas and not simply about enjoyment?"

"I do enjoy Christmas, and I enjoy the preparations for it. But I do so because it brings people together, not to mention the fact that it reminds us of everything we have to be grateful for. So yes, I am absolutely sure that it is about the spirit of Christmas, and not simply personal enjoyment."

"I think you do not understand me any more than I understand you, Rosalind. And I am not sure that I am inclined to explain myself," he said, and although his voice was serious, he spoke gently.

"Then we ought to leave it at that, Gabriel. I have finished gathering all the greenery I need, at any rate, so I shall bid you good day, sir." She hoped that he would simply turn and leave.

"How are you going to get this back to the house?" he said, changing the subject successfully.

"I will make two trips," she said defiantly.

"We need not do that, Rosalind." He immediately stooped to gather up a great armload of the freshly snipped evergreens. "Come, I shall walk with you back down to the house."

"As you wish," Rosalind said, wishing that he would just go away.

CHAPTER 5

"*E*verybody looks so wonderful, do they not?" Claudette grinned excitedly as she looked all around the great ballroom at Newfield Hall. "And everybody is wearing a mask. I had wondered if they really would."

"I think everybody likes a masquerade ball, Claudette," Rosalind said, wishing she had chosen a better mask for herself.

While her dainty little golden mask was very pretty, it also made her nose itch dreadfully. But she had been so busy in the last days that she had not even bothered to try the thing on before the night of the ball itself, and thought ruefully that if she had, she might have been able to make some little alteration that would have made her night a little more comfortable.

"Thank you so much for everything you have done to help me."

"But Claudette, you really have done most of the hard work yourself."

"I really did enjoy putting together those decorations out in the cold outhouse." She looked at her gloved hands for a moment. "But I thank goodness for long white gloves." She laughed.

"Yes, it is quite a danger working with holly." Rosalind laughed too, knowing that her forearms bore a scratch or two, despite the heavy gloves that both women had worn over the last two days as they had spent many long hours preparing a vast array of beautiful adornments to be brought into each of their homes on Christmas Eve.

"I was so excited to show Papa what I had made that I very nearly raced into the house carrying one of the garlands," she said and winced. "It was only when my foot was almost over the threshold that I remembered that it is unlucky to bring the greenery into the house before Christmas Eve. Really, I nearly tripped over there and then." Claudette was so sweet that Rosalind could not help but laugh. "But I managed to turn around at the last minute and raced back to the outhouse to set the garland down with the others again"

"It was very close then." Rosalyn was still laughing.

"It was. But I think it is a measure of my peculiar excitement this Christmas. I have always enjoyed it, but I think having you here to help me make it special this year has made me appreciate it all the more. I feel like a child again."

"What a very good show you two ladies have put on, a very good show," the Duke said as he approached them. "Tell me, are you both enjoying it?"

"I am enjoying it very much, Papa," Claudette said lovingly. "And I had never imagined that I would, I was so afraid of tackling it all."

"I know, my dear" he replied and kissed the top of his daughter's dark brown hair. "But I knew you could manage it. You just needed to have faith in yourself. That is all."

"Good evening, Rosalind." Gabriel appeared at her side, wearing such a simple black eye mask that she almost laughed at his lack of enthusiasm.

"Good evening...... *Gabriel?*" she said a little distantly. "Forgive me, I hardly recognized you with so elaborate a disguise this evening."

"I see you are as confrontational as ever," he said quietly, keeping an eye on his father and sister to be sure that they were still happily engaged in their own conversation.

"Not confrontational, Gabriel, just ready to defend myself as always in your company of late."

"Am I really so bad?" He laughed. "After all, I did come all this way to bring you a cup of spiced wine," he said, and she looked down to see that he was, indeed, holding a cup in each hand. "Here." He handed one to her.

"Thank you," Rosalind said, and felt a little diminished by her behavior.

But, of course, she was only acting from experience. Gabriel had been nothing but standoffish from the moment he had returned from Europe. It was true, of course, that Rosalind had not known him particularly well before he went. Between Eton and then Oxford, Gabriel had already been away from home a good deal before he had even crossed the English Channel.

But what she did remember about him was very different. He had been a pleasant young man, shy, but nice. She could not help but wonder exactly what his life in Europe had been like to make him so very sullen and jaded.

"Your mask is very pretty, Rosalind." He seemed suddenly a little awkward.

"Thank you," she said, and felt awkward herself. "But in all honesty, it makes my nose itch. I am not sure how I will make it through to the end of the night."

"Can you not simply take it off?" he said, and beamed a smile as if pleased with himself for such a brilliant idea.

"And be the only person at the ball not entering into the spirit of it? No, I could not possibly," she said and then smiled mischievously. "After all, I *am* the very spirit of Christmas, am I not?"

"About that, Rosalind." He began, seeming awkward once more. "I had made my way over here to apologize for my behavior."

"Indeed?" Now that she was about to receive the apology that she had previously expected, Rosalind was not entirely sure that she really wanted it at all.

She could sense his discomfort, and she suddenly did not want to prolong it. Just by what he had said so far, he had told her most exactly that he regretted his words to her, perhaps even his disdainful attitude. And that was enough, as far as she was concerned. Rosalind did not want to drag it out any longer but, at the same time, could not see a way of putting a stop to it.

"Yes, I am very sorry for the things I said to you. I had no need to be so rude."

"And I am sorry for the things that I said to you, Gabriel. I am not innocent in all of this; that much I know. I should not have called you *cynical*, it was wrong."

"No, it was right." Gabriel gave her a shy smile, one that reminded her more of the young man he had been before he left for Europe. A young man who was just a little more unsure of himself, than the one who had returned. "I *have* become a little cynical. But I think I have been determined to be so. I have no other means of registering my displeasure at returning home, you see."

"Are you really so displeased?"

"I had not wanted to return, at least not yet," he said and took a sip of the warm wine. "Although I am pleased to see my father and sister again."

"Forgive me for my intrusion, sir, but I am not sure that your father and sister are aware of that."

"You seek to chastise me again, Rosalind?"

"No, not chastise, Gabriel," she said thoughtfully. "Just inform, perhaps?"

"You must think me the most dreadful boar," he said and peered down into his wine glass for a moment before looking back up at her.

His pale blue eyes, against the darkness of his hair in the blackness of his mask, seemed so very clear that she held his gaze for a few moments longer than she ordinarily might have done.

"No, I do not think that," Rosalind said, wondering at her sudden change of heart. She could feel her antagonism towards him slowly evaporating, and it gave her a tiny frisson of panic. "I think you are just in need of a little time to settle into life here again, that is all."

"You think it that simple?"

"I do not think that a simple thing at all, Gabriel. I have no doubt that it is a very difficult thing to walk out of a life that you have grown used to, back into a life that is unlikely to be just as you remember it. It must be a most disorientating experience and I do not think that it is something to be taken lightly."

"They are very fine words, Rosalind," he said with a laugh. "So, you do not think me a lost cause entirely?"

"I do not think you are lost cause at all." She laughed, trying to break the curious little spell which she seemed suddenly to be under.

Rosalind really did feel a little disconcerted that the antagonism between them seemed to be lessening. Mostly because she wondered if she would be better placed to hang onto it for a little while. After all, Gabriel was starting to become more attractive to her and Rosalind could not imagine *that* would be a particularly easy path to follow. Especially when Gabriel was likely to be in very high demand once he had settled back into Duchy life.

"Well, that is something, is it not?" He smiled at her again and Rosalind wished with all her heart that she was not so affected by it.

"Yes, it is. And perhaps it will enable you to enjoy a little something of Christmas after all."

"Well, perhaps just one day at a time, Rosalind."

CHAPTER 6

"*I* must say, I am getting some fearful scratches again," Claudette said as she walked across the impressive black-and-white checkerboard tiled floor of the entrance hall.

"But Claudette, where are your gloves?" Rosalind asked, looking all about for any sign of them. "You will be cut to ribbons."

"Oh, look, here they are," she said with an absent-minded laugh as she hurriedly laid the holly and ivy garland she was carrying down on a side table whilst she put her gloves back on again.

As the two women worked to make the entrance hall look beautiful with their expertly crafted garlands and wreaths, two footmen hovered about them with a wooden step ladder and a handful of tools, anything they might need to be able to help the young ladies hang the decorations.

"I say, this all looks very well indeed." The Duke said, striding through the entrance hall with Gabriel at his side. "What a fine job the two of you have done. I can hardly think I have ever seen such well-made decorations in all my days. Newfield Hall has never looked so festive."

"Papa, that is very sweet." Claudette said and raced to his side, taking one of his mighty hands into her gloved own. "Do you want to see the ones that I made?" Her face was so pink with excitement that Rosalind thought Claudette look like a little girl again.

"Claudette, Father and I have work to do." Gabriel said a little seriously.

"Yes, and it is work that you have not cared for all morning, Gabriel." The Duke looked less than impressed. "Quite why you suddenly feel the need to avoid distraction is beyond me."

"For a start, I made the holly wreath on the front door, Papa." Claudette carried on as if she had not heard her brother at all, and Rosalind felt proud of her friend for choosing to no longer be affected by his moods.

"Well, let me have a closer look, Claudette." The Duke enthusiastically grabbed tightly to his daughter's hand, and the two of them walked out of the hall to inspect her hard work.

"I suppose I have just done it again, have I not?" Gabriel said with a sigh.

"Really, do you not *know* you are doing it? I mean, do you not think about what you are going to say before it comes out? Surely, you could stop it." Rosalind felt a little of the old antagonism returning and felt quite grateful for it.

"I *do* know that I am doing it, Rosalind. Unfortunately, it is not until I have spoken that I immediately come to regret it.

There now, do you have a remedy for that particular problem, I wonder?" he said, a little sarcastically.

"Yes, I do." Rosalind said confidently. "You will simply have to think a little further ahead than us mere mortals."

"Well, I daresay I deserved that." He grimaced a little.

"I daresay you did," she said, but could not help smiling at him.

"Well, why not show me what you have made, since my sister is getting all the attention from the Duke." He seemed to relax just a little and, Rosalind was sure, she could detect a little regret at his initial response.

Perhaps it really was more difficult to settle back into life at home than she had imagined. Rosalind wondered if she had not truly given the matter very much thought and, when Gabriel had told her that she had spoken very fine words on the subject, he might well have been right. Perhaps it was time to try to understand a little, instead of always choosing the path towards argument.

"I have made one or two of the garlands that you see here, and here." She pointed up at them. "But really, Claudette has made most of your family's decorations herself. She was very good, actually, picking the skill up very quickly indeed."

"Indeed. But I must say, your garlands really are very nicely done. Quite excellent."

"I thank you," Rosalind said and wondered why it was that whenever their conversation turned from antagonistic to more relaxed and friendly, she felt a little more unsettled. "And I made this, of course." She pointed up at an artistically arranged ball of ivy, mistletoe, and rosemary. "A kissing bough."

"But it looks like a ball," he said with a look of confusion. "It does not look like a bough at all. Is that not a kissing *ball?*" He began to laugh.

"Are you mocking my kissing bough?" Rosalind said and laughed herself, relaxing a little.

"I would not dream of it," he said and bowed, a look of mischief suddenly crossing his handsome features. "But it really is a ball, Rosalind, you yourself must see it."

"Of course, it is a ball, Gabriel," she said with amused exasperation. "It did not simply turn out round by accident. I made it that way."

"Then you agree that it is a kissing *ball,* and not a kissing *bough?*"

"But the thing is called a kissing bough, whatever shape one chooses to make it."

"You may call it what you wish, Rosalind, but I shall choose to call it the kissing ball." He grinned at her and then looked sideways as his father and sister returned.

"Be careful you do not actually stand under that thing with my brother, Rosalind," Claudette said brightly, and everybody laughed, Gabriel included.

"You think that so terrible a fate, Claudette?" Gabriel was still laughing, and Claudette's face was a picture.

She looked absolutely thrilled to be sharing a joke with her brother at long last and after so many years. For a moment, Rosalind was afraid that Claudette might cry tears of joy, unable to halt the flow of emotion.

"Oh, I had quite forgotten," Rosalind said, desperate to strike up a little conversation for Claudette's sake. "Somebody still needs to select a Yule log."

"A Yule log?" Gabriel asked, almost as if he had never heard of it before.

"Yes, it is Christmas Eve, after all. Today, a Yule log ought really to be brought into the house, you see, and set to burn for the twelve days of Christmas. Really, Europe must be a godforsaken place." She smiled at him and shook her head amusingly.

"I do remember Yule logs, Rosalind, I just do not remember my family particularly bothering about them." He shrugged defensively.

"Well, we shall bother this year," The Duke said with a smile. "And I think *you* should go out and choose one, Gabriel. And please, do not insist that we return to work when you have not enjoyed it for a moment all day long." He laughed.

"I really do not think that I would come back with the right sort of log. I am led to believe that Christmas is a very complicated affair which must be approached scientifically. One might be better off sending Rosalind. Rosalind knows about this sort of thing," he said and turned to look at her, his pale blue eyes finding hers and making her feel just a little unsettled again.

"Alright, you must go together. Rosalind can choose it, and you can carry it. There, any objection will just make you seem ungentlemanly, Gabriel." The Duke's ruddy face creased into a broad smile as he looked from Rosalind to Gabriel and back again.

Rosalind could not help but think that the Duke had suddenly formed the notion that he would *like* to see the two of them wander off together for a while. And, although she could not say exactly that it was true, the very idea of it made Rosalind's cheeks flush a little and she hoped that nobody present could see it.

"Oh, well, I must succumb to my fate," Gabriel said with more alacrity than she had heard him use in his family's company since his return. "And resign myself to an afternoon of being bossed around."

"Right, well, I shall … err, fetch my … my … err, cloak." Rosalind stuttered suddenly, a little tongue-tied.

"But do not be long, the two of you," Claudette said happily. "You do not want to miss the medieval banquet tonight." And she laughed.

"Fear not, sister," Gabriel said and waved at one of the footmen to collect their cloaks. "I do not think that Rosalind could stand so much of my company as to make her late for the evening's festivities."

Rosalind, still a little tongue-tied, could do no more than politely laugh.

CHAPTER 7

*C*laudette smiled at the driver as he helped her down from the carriage in front of Leighton Hall. "Oh, I do so love a Christmas morning walk."

Rosalind and Claudette had agreed to meet very early on Christmas morning, as soon as breakfast was done, to enjoy a frosty walk in the woods of the Leighton estate. At first, they had tried to entreat their families to join them, but it appeared that they all deemed it too early, given that the previous evening had been spent enjoying the festive medieval banquet.

But the young women were much hardier and their excitement at the success of the evening before seemed to energize them further still.

"So do I Claudette. And what a beautiful morning it is too." The two women briefly embraced as they wished each other a very Merry Christmas. "If a little cold."

"It is some degrees cooler than cold, I think." Claudette

laughed as the two women walked, arm in arm, towards the woodland.

A sheen of thin crisp white frost covered the landscape, the leaves of the evergreens looking almost as if they had been made from glass. It was Rosalind's favorite time of the year and she thought that even the beauty of summer could not begin to compete with the beauty of a frosty winter day.

She simply adored the feeling of her cold cheeks and nose, whilst her hands remained warm in her thick, fur gloves. It made her feel very alive, almost a part of the woodland itself.

"Well, let me be the first to declare that last night was a resounding success, Claudette. You should be very proud of yourself, my dear."

"I must admit, I am a little." Claudette gave her shy smile. "But I could not have done any of it without you."

"But you must know that you did the vast majority of the work yourself."

"But I would not have had the confidence to do so without you there," she said quietly. "And did you see their faces when they saw the banquet itself? My father's staff really did put a good deal of work into it. It really did look medieval, did it not?"

"Yes, I think everybody present was quite transported by it all."

"And forgive me for not saying so last night, Rosalind, but you really did look very beautiful in that gown. Have you had it recently made? I am sure that I have never seen you wear it before."

"Yes, it is the first time that I have worn it," Rosalind said, grateful for the praise. "And I thank you, for I was not too sure of the color at first."

Rosalind had a very fair complexion although her hair was a deep golden color. Her brown eyes, large and bright, always made her think of herself suited to only a very few colors. She tended to keep to light colors; ivories and pale greens and pinks. But, as a result of her mother's enthusiastic prodding, she had chosen a fabric in a rich plum shade. It was the color of mulled wine and she had wondered if it would be a little dark for her. But, when she had looked at her reflection in the mirror before setting off for the banquet the night before, Rosalind had been amazed at how it transformed her. The contrast gave her something of a glamorous and dramatic air that she did not normally sport, and she had been a little excited by the change.

"Not at all, that deep shade suits you very well indeed. I think you gathered many an admirer last night, if you do not mind me saying so."

"Goodness, do you really think so?" Rosalind asked, entirely surprised.

"Yes, I do. But I could see you had not noticed at all." Claudette laughed. "You were far too busy making sure that everybody had a wonderful night and that my banquet was as big a success as you had declared it would be. So busy, in fact, that you could not see the admiring glances."

"In truth, I did not see a single one." Rosalind laughed as they made their way deeper into the woods.

The idea of being admired was not entirely distasteful to her; that was true. But she could not help but wonder who exactly had admired her, she felt sure that her heart was beginning to tend in a certain direction, one which would exclude other young men entirely.

"Well, there was Hugo Bentley, for a start," Claudette said cheerfully. "He stared so much that I thought he might trip over his own feet at one point."

"Oh, dear me, Hugo stares at *every* young lady. I can hardly think that he singled me out, for his eyes dart this way and that at every event he attends." Rosalind laughed heartily, thoroughly enjoying herself. "I would dare bet that I was one of *ten* women he fixed his attention on last night."

"That might be true, Rosalind, but he certainly gave you more attention than he gave the other nine."

"Oh, Claudette, you are funny."

"And then there was Hugh Kensington," Claudette said approvingly. "And he really could not take his eyes off you all night, truly."

"Well, I must say that I did not notice at all." Rosalind replied, and wondered if Hugh Kensington really had looked her way at all. "Claudette, are you quite sure that these young men were not looking at you?"

"Absolutely sure. For you see, Austin Lockwood paid me a good deal of attention from afar, and I was certain of it. So, I know that the others were paying their silent attentions to you without a doubt."

"Well, who shall I choose? Hugo or Hugh?" Rosalind giggled girlishly.

"There was, of course, one other who could not seem to turn

his attention away from you." Claudette spoke quietly, almost as though there were someone else within earshot.

"And who was that?" Rosalind asked, her heart beginning to beat just a little faster.

"Gabriel." Claudette whispered loudly, and instinctively looked behind her, almost as if she expected him to be standing there.

"Your brother, Gabriel?" Rosalind said, although she felt a little ridiculous because he was the only man in attendance last night of that name.

"Yes, of course, my brother." Claudette laughed. "Really, I think he has become quite taken with you."

"I cannot imagine that is true, Claudette. After all, we seem to do nothing but argue with one another all the time."

"Perhaps not all the time." Claudette said gently. "And I think, perhaps, that your argumentative streak has done much to dissuade my brother from his determined dissatisfaction."

"Well, he does seem to have settled down a little bit, but I cannot claim any credit for that. I am sure it is simply that he has come to realize how much he missed you and your father when he was away."

Rosalind thought back to the day that she and Gabriel had been cutting holly on the Newfield estate. He had told her then that he had been pleased to see his father and sister again, and she had wanted to tell him to find some way of telling them so. She had hinted at it, but she had not had the courage at the time to say it fully.

"He is certainly softening, Rosalind, and I think that we really do have you to thank for that. For some reason, he seems to listen to you. I think it is because you have the courage to go back at him, to stand up for yourself when he behaves badly. He respects you for it, and I think, *I truly think*, that he has come to regard you quite highly."

"Well, I do not know what to say." Rosalind felt her cheeks flush scarlet.

"Well, you are blushing, so that is a good sign."

"I am not blushing, Claudette, it is just the coldness of the day."

"I do not believe you for a minute." Claudette said and laughed. "But I am glad that you are blushing. It means that you like my brother too, and that would make me very happy indeed."

"Well, I do not want you to get your hopes up. And, in truth, I would not be keen to get my own hopes up either," Rosalind said honestly. "After all, a young man who is one day to be a Duke is often something of a draw to the most beautiful ladies for several miles around. I daresay that he will soon discover that he is greatly in demand."

"And you think that he might find himself very distracted sooner or later?"

"He is only human, as are we all." Rosalind laughed.

"Yes, but if you had seen him continually eyeing the kissing bough last night, especially whenever you were near it, you might think differently."

"The kissing ball? I mean, bough?"

"Yes, I am certain that he hoped to find the two of you suddenly underneath it at the same time."

"My dear Claudette, I had no idea that you were such a romantic."

"Neither did I." She laughed as the two of them turned to make their way back towards the carriage. "But I am still certain of what I saw, Rosalind. And I am certain that my brother has come to have some very strong feelings for you."

CHAPTER 8

*A*fter a thoroughly wonderful Christmas day spent with her family, and a St Stephen's Day morning, in which she had gleefully presented the household servants with the presents that she had chosen herself, Rosalind found herself a little excited to be returning to Newfield Hall.

As part of the Christmas celebrations, Claudette had been very keen on the idea of spending some of their time in charity, to give thanks for everything that they had enjoyed throughout the festive season.

The carriage ride over was the first time that Rosalind had been truly able to think about everything that she and Claudette had discussed the morning before. Could it be true that Gabriel really had taken a liking to her? And yet he seemed to start every conversation in so antagonistic a manner that, at times, she could not begin to imagine that it could be true.

But what she *did* know for certain was that she had been fighting an attraction for him almost from the very first.

There was something about his dissatisfaction which seemed to her to set him apart a little, to make him seem a lonely figure. And, for all his light animosity, she could not help but think that all he needed was a way to settle back into his old life.

Rosalind arrived at Newfield just in time to see the Duke handing over the presents that Claudette, following Rosalind's lead, had chosen for their own staff. And she had chosen very well indeed, taking good account of the personalities of each and every servant.

One of the second footmen looked overjoyed to receive a beautifully illustrated book about garden birds. It was, apparently, one of his greatest passions. Each and every gift was well received, and the effort to get just the right gift seemed greatly appreciated by all.

"Well, it looks as if you have had a wondrous effect on our staff too, does it not?" Gabriel said after sidling up to her. "You really *are* the spirit of Christmas."

"Mock me if you must, Gabriel, but you must know that your sister chose these gifts. I had no hand in this at all, except to say that she should make it all very individual."

"And she has, to great effect, I would say."

"Yes, she has done very well indeed." Rosalind said and felt proud of Claudette.

He calmly said, "and now, I understand, I am to be carted about the county delivering little charity boxes to the needy." Rosalind was pleased to note that he did not seem at all disdainful about the idea.

If he had been so, Rosalind would have been greatly disappointed. As much as she did not like to get her hopes up, she could not help but think it a possibility, albeit a distant one, that there may be some truth in what Claudette had said.

But if she had discovered that Gabriel Blackwood was an uncharitable man, a man who truly did not appreciate his own privileges in life enough to understand the life of the person who lacked those privileges, it would have changed her opinion of him almost entirely.

"Yes, Claudette mentioned that she would be enlisting your help." Rosalind added. "I do hope that you do not mind."

"I do not mind at all," he said with an uncharacteristically warm smile. "Especially if I take the smaller carriage with you, whilst my father and Claudette take the other."

"We are to go in separate carriages?"

"Yes, we have a good deal of ground to cover today." He laughed. "Not to mention that each carriage is already well packed with many boxes."

"Oh, very wise. Of course, we would not all fit into one carriage with everything we need to carry. I say, Claudette really has got the hang of this now, has she not?"

"She is quite the spirit of organization."

"Oh, she is not the spirit of Christmas then?" Rosalind said mischievously.

"No, that honor still remains yours." He gave her a slow smile and looked pointedly into her eyes for several moments. "Stop looking for a fight, Rosalind."

"All right, I surrender." she said, and held her hands up, palms forward. "I shall not argue with you all day, Gabriel."

"Oh, now, do not take all the fun out of it." he said with a comical frown. "I think I'd rather like to have a little row with you now and again."

"That is just perverse, Gabriel."

"No, not perverse, you are very… it's just, interesting."

"Right, come along then, let us get to the carriages," The Duke said, already warmly wrapped against the cold of the day.

"Yes, off we go," Claudette said, barely able to contain herself.

As they went their separate ways, agreeing to meet up at Newfield Hall again for some leftover plum pudding and hot ale, Rosalind felt very content indeed.

And it was not just the idea that she was to spend a couple of hours in Gabriel's company, but also the idea that they would be doing something to improve the lives of others, even if only for that day.

Each of the boxes contained good food, including a decent portion of cooked meat, some plum pudding, some cheese, and some pieces of fruit. And there was enough of it to give a poor family a very good meal for St Stephen's Day, a treat that they would not otherwise be expecting.

"Right, shall I operate the list, or would you like to do it?" he asked, holding out a piece of paper upon which Claudette had listed the name and address of each recipient of their Christmas charity.

"Oh, your sister handed *you* the responsibility, Gabriel. I would not seek to interfere in any way."

"Even though you are so very good at this sort of thing?"

"You are mocking me again, Gabriel."

"No, I would not dream of it," he laughed.

When they arrived outside the first of the little houses to which charity was to be given, Rosalind could sense Gabriel's unwanted discomfort.

She realized that it was unlikely he had ever done anything like this before; hands-on charity always seemed to be a task more easily performed by women. For a moment, she wondered if there was a reason for that. Perhaps men struggled with the emotions that would undoubtedly arise from such an act. And yet, he jumped down from the carriage determinedly, and turned to help her down too before lifting out one of the boxes.

That he was determined to see the whole thing through, not just wait in the carriage whilst she delivered the parcel, made her heart warm towards him all the more.

As Gabriel stood holding the box, Rosalind tapped lightly on the ramshackle wooden door.

"Good morning, Mrs. Benson," Rosalind said brightly when the door slowly opened inwards. "Forgive the intrusion, but we have come to deliver a gift from the Duke of Newfield and his family."

"A gift?" The aging woman said, her grey eyes seeming to brighten instantly. "A gift from the Duke himself, you say?"

"Yes, it is just a few treats for you and your family for St Stephen's Day, Mrs. Benson. May you enjoy them and have a very fine Christmas indeed."

"Thank you, Lady Rosalind." Mrs. Benson said, blinking hard as her eyes filled with tears. "Really, what a lovely thing to do.

And please do thank His Grace for us, won't you?" she said and smiled at Gabriel as he handed her the box.

With the encounter over, Rosalind and Gabriel made their way back to the carriage in silence. Gabriel helped her in and she thanked him, and then he climbed into the carriage himself and sat at her side.

"Are you alright, Gabriel?" she asked cautiously.

"Yes, thank you." he said and paused for a moment before continuing. "I suppose I had not really given a good deal of thought to quite how something so simple can make such a difference to another person. Really, it is not just the food, is it? It is the idea that one has been thought of."

"Yes, it is very simple."

"And I feel very humbled by it. How disdainful I have been of the *simplicity* of life and Christmas back here in England. And now I have been shown that it is the simple things in life which sometimes mean the most. I am not sure if it is you or Claudette, but somebody has certainly taught me a lesson today, have they not?"

"And that, my dear Gabriel, is the spirit of Christmas," Rosalind said with a warm smile and, before she had a chance to stop herself, she reached out and patted his hand. "Well, we ought to keep moving if we are to make it back in time for plum pudding and hot ale," she said brightly.

"Yes, we must."

CHAPTER 9

"*I* can hardly believe that twelfth night is finally here. Christmas really has been a success here at Newfield Hall, has it not?" Claudette said with a rosy-cheeked smile full of pride for her hard work and excitement for the night ahead.

"That is the mark of a very good Christmas, Claudette. One that is so full of fun and good cheer that it passes by all too quickly." Rosalind was greatly looking forward to the night ahead. "Well done, Claudette. Really, well done indeed."

"Ah, here is my dear Rosalind." The Duke came towards her with his hands outstretched. "And what a treat you look this evening, my dear. How lovely you look."

"Your Grace, you say that every time I see you." Rosalind laughed.

"Ah, but it is true, is it not, Gabriel?" He turned to his son who had come to join them.

"It most certainly is true," Gabriel said deeply, which made Rosalind blush.

She really would have to find a way to stop her cheeks flushing in his company, or else he would certainly discover her true feelings for him. To make matters worse, Claudette gave her what she obviously thought was a secret look. It was, however, anything but, and Rosalind was certain that she saw a smile of amusement flicker briefly on Gabriel's lips.

Gabriel looked just about as handsome as she had ever seen him on that night. He wore full black, with neatly tailored breeches and tailcoat, and gleaming black knee boots. His waistcoat was a pale cream, and he looked very smart indeed. His dark brown hair was thick, and his pale blue eyes seemed clearer than ever. How had she not realized before what a truly handsome man Gabriel Blackwood was?

"Well, who is looking forward to the games this evening?" Rosalind said in a bid to shatter the awkward silence. "I know I am."

"Are we to play games?" Gabriel asked, in a brief return to his former disdain.

"You most certainly are, Gabriel," Claudette said bravely. "I have put together so many fun things for us to do and I insist that you try them all."

"Yes, as do I," Rosalind chimed in to back her friend.

"Well, Father, it looks as if I would not do myself any great favors by refusing, does it not?"

"I hardly think you would survive it, my dear boy." The Duke laughed, and it was a wonderful, deep, rumbling noise.

The tension of the last weeks seemed to have eased greatly and Rosalind knew in her heart that it was the renewed father-son relationship between them.

They had finally come to reclaim everything that had once been theirs; three years before when they had, by the necessity of Gabriel's grand tour, become estranged. Over that time, Rosalind thought how easy it would be to think of the silliest things, little arguments that had never quite been settled, differences of opinion and suchlike. Little things that would undoubtedly grow out of all proportion when one was alone in a foreign country, maybe even turning close relations into near strangers.

Who knew what really happened when a person was away from their family for so long? Rosalind certainly did not.

But what she knew for certain was that it was pure *joy* for her to see the Blackwood family so mended. All three of them looked comfortable and happy; they seemed to glow in their newfound friendship for one another. All in all, Gabriel had come a long way in a very short space of time and she wondered how long it would be before he fully took his place in society again and began to turn heads with that handsome face of his.

"I am inclined to agree, Father," Gabriel laughed. "Well, I am at your disposal, ladies. I will play whatever silly game you choose for me."

"Then I choose snapdragon for you, brother," Claudette said, her face a picture of excited mischief.

"Snapdragon?" Gabriel winced. "Oh, must I?"

"You do remember Snapdragon, then?" Rosalind said brightly.

"Yes, yes, I do, unfortunately, only too well."

"I think my brother is afraid to burn his fingers," Claudette said teasingly.

"Yes, I am." Gabriel was laughing heartily, his handsome features lit up by it. "Not to mention my tongue."

Claudette had prepared many games for the evening, but the most exciting of them all was undoubtedly, Snapdragon. It was not for the fainthearted, consisting of a great metal dish full of brandy which had been set alight. Floating in the brandy were raisins, which one had to quickly pluck out with one's fingers and cool down in one's mouth. Whilst it caused a good deal of excitement at any gathering, there were always more people who abstained than actually played.

"But, in the spirit of Christmas," he said and looked pointedly at Rosalind. "I shall only play it if Rosalind will play it."

"What?" Rosalind shrieked. "No, I do not want to play."

"Well, I had never thought to see such a protest." He laughed, as did the rest of the party.

"Rosalind, you must, you really must," Claudette said, barely able to contain her excitement. The poor woman was almost jumping up and down on the spot. "And do not forget, the person who picks the most raisins not only wins, but will undoubtedly meet their true love in the coming year."

"If you believe such poppycock," Rosalind said, laughing and absolutely desperate not to play.

"Good heavens, it would seem that the spirit of Christmas has just evaporated," Gabriel said with a taunting laugh. "Well, if you are afraid to play against me, so be it."

"Oh no, absolutely not," Rosalind said, taking the bait with both hands. "Not only will I play, Gabriel Blackwood, but I will certainly pick out more raisins than you do."

"Excellent," he said and clapped his hands together. "Now that is *spirit* if you like. Although it is, perhaps, a little too fierce to be called Christmas spirit." He smiled at her and then, she was absolutely certain of it, his eyes strayed to the kissing bough which hung just outside the great doors of the ballroom.

When he looked back at her, his smile had faded, and his look had become something much more intense. Rosalind made to speak, but could think of absolutely nothing to say. In the end, all she could do was smile at him and hope that he did not see how deeply she blushed.

The evening had gone wonderfully, with squeals of delight as people bobbed for apples and tried, often failing, to throw wooden hoops over metal pins. There really was a great atmosphere, with everybody taking part in at least something, and doing it with gusto.

When the time came for the Snapdragon, a great crowd had gathered around the bowl. Several men and only two brave young ladies, one of whom was Rosalind, had decided to play.

As soon as the game began, and the first raisin was plucked from the bowl, the excited chatter of the crowd grew. When Rosalind plucked out her first raisin, she shrieked as the scorching little fruit burnt her fingers. When she hurriedly popped it into her mouth to cool it down, she was almost cross-eyed with the heat. Gabriel, watching her intently, laughed so hard that his pale blue eyes shone.

"I say, well done, Rosalind." He called at the top of his voice before reaching into the bowl to pluck at the first of his raisins.

As fierce as the competition was in the beginning, in the end it seemed that only Rosalind and Gabriel remained. They had both become very determined, both enjoying themselves so much, and the bowl was soon empty of raisins.

When the raisins they had each collected had been counted, and then recounted at Gabriel's insistence, it was established that Rosalind had won the Snapdragon by a single raisin. She was absolutely gleeful, smiling so broadly at Gabriel that her jaw ached. But she could not stop smiling, she had truly never had so much fun in years.

"Well, it looks as if you are all set to meet your one true love in the coming year. I do hope he is worth the burnt fingers and the scorched tongue, my dear," Gabriel said quietly into her ear.

"Do you really believe in that sort of thing, Gabriel?" She laughed. "After all, you are a man of the world; a man of sense. I would think you would know better."

"I know better *now*, that is for certain." He smiled and bowed. "I think I now know better than I ever did."

CHAPTER 10

"So, now that it is all over for another year, did you have a lovely time, my dear?" Lady Beatrice asked when the two of them were alone in the drawing room at Leighton Hall the following day.

"I must admit that I think it was my favorite yuletide ever. Perhaps it was because I was involved in even more organizing, and Christmas events than usual, given that I was helping Claudette."

"You really do love this time of year, do you not?" Lady Beatrice looked at her lovingly.

"I cannot begin to tell you how much I love it, Mama. It is a magical time for me and it always has been."

"I know, you have been the same since you were a child." Lady Beatrice rose from the little couch to take a turn about the room, lightly touching her daughter's golden hair as she passed. "But I do hope you do not feel suddenly flat now that it is all over."

"I suppose I do a little, Mama, but nothing that I shall not get over." She smiled warmly.

"Oh, I say." Lady Beatrice said, crossing to the window and peering out of it. "It looks as if we have company, my dear. The Duke's carriage approaches."

"Oh, really?" Rosalind suddenly rose to her feet, quickly putting a hand up to her hair to make sure that all was well.

"My dear girl, he is obviously smitten with you already. You need not panic suddenly about your hair." Lady Beatrice gave her a knowing smile.

"Mama, really." Rosalind tried to sound exasperated. "It might not be Gabriel anyway. It might just be the Duke himself."

"No, it is Gabriel." Lady Beatrice was still peeking out of the window. "And his dear sister. Oh, I do love Claudette."

"Mama, you must come away from the window. What if they see you?"

"Well, sit yourself down, my dear. They will be with us in a moment, I am sure."

When the butler showed Gabriel and Claudette into the drawing room, Lady Beatrice did a wonderful job of looking surprised to see them.

"Oh, how wonderful," she said quickly rising to her feet to receive Claudette warmly. "My dear Carlton, would you be so kind as to have some tea sent up to us all?" she called over Claudette's shoulder to the butler.

"Very well, My Lady," the butler said and bowed a little before leaving the room.

"I wonder if perhaps Rosalind would care for a stroll around the garden? I know how she likes her frosty walks," Gabriel said and seemed nervous, despite trying to appear nonchalant and amusing.

"Yes, I am sure she would like that very much." Lady Beatrice answered for her daughter in a way which made Rosalind squint at her.

Still, since she really *did* want to take a turn about the garden with Gabriel, she made no complaint.

"How are your fingertips this afternoon?" Gabriel asked the moment the two of them were outside and walking the little gravel path around the immaculate oval lawn.

"A little bit sore, if I am honest," she said, and pulled her hand from her fur glove to show him the reddened skin of her thumb and forefinger.

"The same," he said with a laugh as he held out his hand to show the same little injuries.

"What fools are we for playing such a game, but it was still very exciting."

"And I really did want all the raisins," he said with a grin. "Because, you see, I thought it might be nice for me to meet my one true love this year."

"But it is I who will have that, now." Rosalind laughed nervously, she was so sure now that everything Claudette had said was true.

"Unless, of course, your one true love is me, in which case I need not have bothered to even play at all."

"I think that might be far too logical to be romantic, Gabriel."

"I suspect you are right. But still, I am pleased that you recognized my attempt to be romantic, regardless."

"Yes, I recognized your attempt."

"And you are not displeased by it?" He raised his eyebrows and looked at her hopefully, once again reminding her of the shy young man he had once been.

"Not at all, Gabriel." Rosalind felt a little light-headed, and suddenly moved, very romantic, and very much in love.

"I have enjoyed getting to know you again," he said, and held out his arm for her to take as they walked. "But I realize that I did not particularly know you very well before I went away." He shrugged.

"No, but we still knew each other, if only a little."

"And I am very glad now that I am back from Europe."

"You do not feel so dissatisfied?"

"I was never really dissatisfied, if I am honest. The truth of the thing is that I did not feel myself ready to learn the role and responsibilities of the Duke. Obviously, providing God's good grace, my father will live a long time. But something about having to come home and prepare for the role that will one day be mine felt dreadfully tying, especially after the freedoms I have enjoyed abroad."

He patted her hand and continued. "I think I had myself convinced that the whole thing would be very dull and, by the time I arrived home again, was absolutely certain of it. Unfortunately, it made me somewhat disagreeable to everyone around me, including you."

"Well, it is all very understandable. You have been away for a good deal of time, and it will take a while for you to settle in. You must be patient with yourself."

"No, I am settled now. I have been settled for some days. But I do not think I would be so, had you not been here to put me straight where others have not dared to. My father is a wonderful man, and so kind and generous that he has done a tremendous job of hiding his disappointment in my behavior these last weeks. And dear Claudette, well, is too sweet to say a word out of place to me. But you, Rosalind, you are quite something else altogether."

"So, I am not sweet?"

"No, you are *not* sweet," he said with a rakish smile. "But if I said you were so, you would surely not have believed me."

"No, I would not." She laughed and acknowledged the veracity of his remark.

"But you are bold, intelligent, and beautiful. And you are so open-hearted and kind, without fear of any sort. All in all, I find that I have begun to fall in love with you."

"Have you really?" she said, her heart thundering away under her great heavy cloak.

"Yes, I have. And I have only one regret in all of this."

"What is that?" Rosalind asked, almost bowled over with sudden worry. What on earth could he be regretting?

"That I was never once able to get you anywhere near that kissing ball thing last night. Try as I might, I just could not seem to edge you in that direction." He smiled at her and she was greatly relieved.

"Oh, I see," she could feel the little blush rising once more.

Gabriel darted a very quick look down the immense lawn towards the house, checking the windows of the drawing room for any sign that her mother or his sister were peering out at them. And then, obviously deeming them to be safe, he quickly pulled her behind a thick box hedging and hurriedly kissed her on the lips.

It was a most wonderful feeling, and so unexpected. And then, almost as quickly as it had begun, it was over, and he had pulled her back out onto the pathway and they resumed their walk back towards the hall.

Rosalind felt warm and dizzy, she held the back of her hand up to her lips as if to try and hide her blushes. She looked up to Gabriel to see the widest, happiest grin she had ever seen. "Gabriel, you caught me so much by surprise."

"I am so sorry, my dear Rosalind. Should I… should I not do it again?" He bore a cheeky grin.

"I don't think it would be suitable to do it ever again." Her face was still rosy but she held a firm stare.

"I…" Gabriel lost his grin. His face showed a little distress. "I… I'm so sorry…"

Rosalind burst out laughing. "Oh, my sweetest Gabriel. I don't think it would be suitable to do it ever again… it's the type of thing only married couples should do."

"Oh, you tease," he cried out aloud and roared with laughter. "In that case, my dear Rosalind." Gabriel spun around in front to face her, lowered himself onto one knee, and took her hands in his. "Rosalind Leighton. Would you do me the greatest honor of becoming my wife?"

"Yes, yes, yes, I would, my sweet Gabriel."

EPILOGUE

"*I* can hardly believe that the daffodils are only just out and we are married already, my dearest Gabriel." Rosalind peered out of the window of her new home, Newfield Hall, the morning after her wedding. "Everything has happened so quickly."

"I hope you do not regret it, my love, for I know that I never shall," he said, and crossed the room to join her, peering down at the huge bed of daffodils, a wide expanse of yellow bloomed from one side to the other.

"No, I do not regret it for one minute. When you love somebody, you know it quite quickly, do you not?"

"I know that I certainly did."

"And you still love me?"

"Of course, I still love you, Rosalind. Really, what a question after less than a day of marriage," he laughed loudly.

"I just thought I would check."

"And you still love me?"

"Of course, I love you, Gabriel. And I always shall."

"And you might love me just a little bit more when you find out where I am taking you for a little trip."

"A little trip?"

"Yes, just a few months away to mark the occasion of our marriage."

"And where are we going?"

"It is not the grand tour that I had, Rosalind, but we shall still visit a great many places," he smiled as she turned to look at him.

"Am I finally going to Europe?" Rosalind asked, her eyes wide.

"Yes, my dear. We are going to Paris, Rome, and Venice. What do you think to that?"

"You know, I do believe that you are right. I think I *do* love you even more." She threw her arms around his neck and he wrapped his arms around her. Their lips met and Europe, for the moment, was forgotten.

THE DUKE, THE EARL, AND THE JOKER PREVIEW

"I must admit, I do get so excited by the twelve days of Christmas. I feel almost as I did when I was a child." Lady Juliet Whitehall spoke quietly as she and her dearest friend took tea in the drawing room of Forbes Hall.

"As do I. I think it is the prospect of so much celebration. I know there are parties and little events throughout the year, but there is certainly something about the Yuletide Season which rivals even the London Season for me. It has a warmth that compares to nothing else." Stella Lawson was nodding in enthusiastic agreement.

"Yes, that is it exactly!" Juliet went on. "There is a warmth. There is a cozy feeling of home and hearth, and friends and family. That is certainly not the case in the London Season.

Both young women, each just turned twenty years, had only attended one London Season and neither had come away from it with the invitations and the matrimonial interest that many other young ladies had received.

Still, it had been only their first, and neither one of them suffered the family pressures that so many other young ladies were forced to endure, a blessing for which both were quietly grateful.

Despite being the eldest daughter of the Earl of Forbes, no pressure had been brought to bear by Juliet's family at all. The Earl was a kindly, jovial sort of a man, one who would never see any of his precious offspring made uncomfortable or anxious by his demands.

"There is none of the expectation, is there?" Stella continued. "I mean, we can think of enjoyment without thinking of finding a good match. It is a time to relax and let go of such things."

"Yes, although Papa is inviting the Duke of Richfield this year." Juliet winced.

"And he has agreed?" Stella's eyes were wide.

"I am afraid so."

"But surely this is a happy event. I know you suffer a certain amount of nerves around the man, but you still hold him in high regard, do you not?"

"Yes, very high. Oh, but I wish I did not. I think it is that high regard which renders me foolish and makes me so clumsy whenever I see him. Not that I have seen him for some time now." Juliet was glad of the opportunity to speak of Edward Burton.

She had been desperate to talk the whole thing out ever since her father had declared himself to have invited the new Duke to the Whitehall Family celebrations.

"And will the Duke be staying here at Forbes Hall for the duration?"

"Yes, Stella. He is, in fact, staying longer than the twelve nights. He is staying a full fortnight and a day from the day before Christmas Eve."

"Goodness!" Stella exclaimed.

"I know, my dear. It is an awfully long time for me to have to behave myself as a normal young lady." As excited as Juliet was, she was equally dismayed by the prospect.

"Oh, Juliet! You are a normal young lady. You are a very fine young lady actually."

"How kind you are. But you know what I mean. You know how I can tend towards bumbling and foolish exclamations."

"But that is only nerves."

"And I shall be nervous for the entire full fortnight and one day!" Juliet laughed despite herself.

"Then we shall find ways to make you less nervous."

"I do not see how that is to be achieved." Juliet rose and walked to the fireplace, pulling the bell to summon the footman. "More tea, I think, if we are to have a long conversation."

"Indeed." Stella laughed.

Juliet and Stella had been the closest of friends since they were children. The Lawson family were the nearest neighbors to Forbes Hall, but it was more than proximity which had held the two women together for so long.

There was a deep understanding between them, and each

harbored a cherished wish that the other would succeed in life and be truly happy. There was none of the thinly veiled competition which Juliet had observed with so many of her acquaintances, and therefore her one true friendship brought her the greatest of comfort.

"So, how are we to make me less nervous?" Juliet said the moment she sat down on the dark green brocade couch next to Stella.

"Well, I think we must first remember that Edward Burton is *just* a man."

"*Just* a man?"

"Yes. He is a man, the same as all the others."

"Aside from being a duke, an older man of two and thirty years with experience of life, with just about the most handsome face I have ever seen in my life?" Juliet sounded incredulous.

"You see, you are talking yourself into believing him to be some sort of deity." Stella shrugged in such an exaggerated way that Juliet laughed loudly. "But please do not snort with laughter in that fashion when you are in his company, whether he be a man *or* a god." Stella smiled as she teased her.

"And that is the very thing, Stella. I cannot seem to control my awkward behavior when he is near me. And now that he is the Duke of Richfield, I am sure it will be even worse. I shall be more nervous than ever."

Edward Burton had lost his father to a very sudden illness in the early spring. He had been made the Duke much sooner than anybody had expected, since his own father had been such a hardy sort of a fellow.

Juliet had attended the funeral, of course. Most of the county had. But her father and Edward's father had been the firmest of friends for as long as Juliet could remember, and she felt her own sense of loss of the man who had once been the Duke of Richfield.

Since then, Juliet had not seen Edward, although her father, the Earl, kept regular contact. She knew that her father felt a certain paternal responsibility towards Edward Burton, even though he had been well prepared for the role of Duke and was a man who was truly old enough to take on his own cares and responsibilities without assistance.

It was in just such a paternal vein that Juliet's father had insisted Edward spend his first Yuletide as Duke under their own roof. He had not wanted the man's first Christmas since the passing of his own father, to be such a dreadfully quiet one. Not, of course, that a duke is ever short on invitations, whatever the time of year, but the Earl particularly wanted Edward to spend the festive season with people who knew him well.

The Duke had few living relatives, none of them were close enough that Christmas might be a comfortable, relaxed affair. And the Duke himself must have felt some sort of relief at the invitation, for it was accepted immediately, according to her father.

"You have not seen him since his father's funeral, is that so?" Stella asked.

"Yes. Oh, and it was such a sad thing." Juliet pouted.

"It was. The old Duke was a fine man." Stella fell quiet for a moment. "But prior to that, what was your last encounter with Edward?"

"It was at the Hartington-Brown's late winter ball in February." Juliet screwed her face up as Stella stifled a laugh. "I see you remember it well!"

"Forgive me," Stella said, her face turning pink from the exertion of holding down her merriment.

"You are forgiven." Juliet laughed. "It was, indeed, the event at which I chose to tell Edward all about the book I was reading so that I might impress him with my intelligence. And then, of course, I re-told the whole thing out of chronological order, confused many of the characters, and only realized I had done so when Edward himself had corrected me."

"Oh yes, he had lately read the same book himself," Stella said quietly.

"And in my sudden haste to be away from him so that he might not see my cheeks flush brightly with embarrassment, I tripped over my own feet and almost fell to the floor of the Hartington-Brown's ballroom."

"But you did not fall entirely," Stella said helpfully.

"No, but only because I had run half the length of the ballroom bent almost double in my determination to remain upright. Really, it was so inelegant that I still think I would have done better to simply let go and flop to the floor."

"Oh, Juliet," Stella said, and finally let go of her laughter. "Forgive me, but it is the way you recount the details which makes me laugh so much."

"Again, you are forgiven," Juliet said with a twinkling smile.

Juliet had a very fine sense of humor, and was certainly not mean-spirited when teased. In fact, she quite enjoyed being teased, as well as a little teasing of her own. She had a spirit of fun and had always found much enjoyment in genuine laughter.

Still, she really did like the Duke very much indeed, and wished whole-heartedly that she could rein in some of her more ridiculous tendencies in his presence. The problem was, she liked him so much that it made her nervous and ever more clumsy, and prone to be either tongue-tied, or unable to stop speaking altogether.

Juliet had nurtured a fondness for Edward for as long as she could remember, but she thought she had been sixteen when the fondness had been tinged with romance. And he was so much older than she, twelve years older, that Juliet had never held the illusion that he would one day see her finer qualities too.

As a matter of fact, she had always fully expected him to ignore her, to dismiss her, a silly girl; one beneath his notice. She was just the daughter of a family friend and that was all, she felt sure. But every time she heard of his successes as the new Duke of Richfield, she found herself wishing that she could see him.

Her contact with Edward had been sporadic over the years and almost always a time of great embarrassment and self-consciousness. Their fathers had met regularly, but their children less so. And there was, of course, a difference in their ages which meant that Edward had been too old to become a particular friend to Juliet's brother, Adam. At two and twenty, Adam was ten years younger and would never have been a credible friend for Edward as they had grown up.

Perhaps Juliet would feel a little different if she and Edward had been of a similar age, or if she had any real experience of life to speak of; something which would render them a little more equal. But, of course, where was a young lady of twenty, who had attended only *one* London Season, to have gathered the sort of experiences that could be talked about?

Juliet sometimes wished that she did not find Edward so very handsome. He had his father's coloring; a tendency towards slightly darker skin but with pale ash-brown hair which seemed almost to have lines of silver in it. His eyes were a pale blue-grey, which sometimes seemed a little cold, especially, it seemed to Juliet, when he regarded *her* in particular.

She knew, of course, that this was her imagination at work. It was her *small* self, telling her that she was certainly not good enough for such a handsome and so accomplished a man. And a man of the world to boot.

In her heart, Juliet wondered if that were the truth. If it was, it would certainly explain her nervousness in his company. She wondered how on earth she was to manage for more than a fortnight.

"It needn't be so fraught with nerves, Juliet. This Yuletide could mark a change, a turn in your circumstances. Perhaps this is cause for excitement rather than fear." Stella had recovered and returned to her dutiful role of helping her friend.

"I wish I could feel just that, Stella," Juliet said when the footman came into the drawing room with a fresh tea tray.

"Well, I shall not leave your side throughout the whole thing, so you may draw some comfort from that at least," Stella said brightly.

"Thank you."

"And we shall just have to wait and see what the festive season brings."

Read The Duke, the Earl, and the Joker a three book regency Christmas box set now.

A RACE AGAINST THE DUKE
PREVIEW

Lady Serena Chamberlain always dipped her head and smiled. She so enjoyed events at the home of Lady Beatrice Wakefield. It wasn't the largest country mansion in Hertfordshire but Serena had always thought it the most welcoming. She had known Lady Beatrice her entire life and had always felt very much at home in her drawing-room.

"Lady Chamberlain, how very nice to see you again."

Serena turned to see Lady Josephine Dalloway, the new Countess of Pennington standing behind her.

The two had met on three previous occasions since Lady Dalloway had been at Pennington Hall and Serena liked her very much indeed. They were of a similar age and Serena found her such easy company.

"Lady Dalloway, how well you look," Serena said and meant it. "I think motherhood must suit you very nicely indeed."

"I get plenty of exercise, at any rate." Lady Dalloway laughed. "Beth has just reached the stage where she can pull herself up to standing and take a few steps. However, she has realized that if she takes very quick steps she can stay upright for just a little longer. It means that the nurse and I seem always to be running to keep up with her before she either falls over or collides with some hard object."

"Oh, how adorable," Serena cooed.

"You really must come over to Pennington Hall and have tea with me one day, Lady Chamberlain. You could see little Beth for yourself."

"I should like that so much, Lady Dalloway," Serena said as her cheeks pinked by the pleasure such an invitation gave her.

Serena did not have many close acquaintances. She assumed that to be because she was such a keen horsewoman, as was her birthright, and she gathered that not many young ladies were particularly interested to hear her talk about it at length. Still, as much as she had tried to modify her conversation just a little, it seemed as if her reputation was already set in stone. While she did not want for invites, they were almost always to larger affairs, rather than smaller, more intimate ones. The idea of being invited into Lady Dalloway's home as a particular friend was something very special to her.

"Perhaps you could call me Josephine." Josephine smiled at her. "After all, I think that you and I are going to be good friends."

"I should like that they much, Josephine. And you must call me Serena. Yes, I think that we are going to be very good friends indeed." Serena smiled brightly. "And if I am entirely honest, Josephine, I do not really have that many."

"I can hardly believe that is true. After all, I find you the most fascinating company."

"How very kind you are. Really, I know I talk a little too much about horses and racing and all the events that I attend, but I do try not to overdo it. I am learning from my mistakes."

"It is never a mistake to be yourself, Serena," Josephine said firmly. "If you only ever have one or two friends in this world, let them be friends who understand you entirely and enjoy your company as it is with no alterations."

"What a lovely thing to say."

"And I mean it, Serena. There are already enough people in society pretending to be anything other than they are. In truth, I think I have just described the clear majority of them. For myself, I find it terribly tiresome to speak to somebody who holds one opinion one week and quite another the following simply because styles and fashions have changed."

"That is very true. It is almost as if it is quite impossible to get to know a person truthfully at all." Serena giggled and covered her mouth with gloved fingers.

"Then let us make a pact today. Let us promise to always be ourselves when we are in company and then we shall both be assured of truly knowing at least one person in our acquaintance." Josephine laughed.

"I think that sounds like a promise I shall easily be able to keep. I really am looking forward to coming to see you at Pennington."

"Then that is settled, we shall have tea next week. What about Wednesday?"

"Oh dear, I am going to be awkward already. Might we make it Thursday? I only ask because I am interviewing a new jockey on Wednesday and I have no idea how long the engagement might last."

"Of course, Thursday suits me perfectly." Josephine smiled as she eyed the trays of neatly cut little sandwiches hungrily. "Is this a new jockey for one of your big races?"

"Yes. Well, we do have a number of small race meets to attend over the coming months, but I am particularly looking for a new jockey for the Wakefield Chase."

"Yes, the Wakefield Chase seems to be awfully important. I must admit, I know very little about horse racing, but I do know that the Wakefield Chase is quite an event."

"Yes, for my family it is probably the most important racing event of the year."

"But you go to so many others, do you not? What makes this one the most important for your family?" Josephine smiled at the maid who stood behind the table of refreshments and the woman immediately set about making up a tea tray for two. "Where would you like to sit?" she added before Serena had even begun to answer her previous questions.

"Let us sit in the afternoon sunshine on the little couch under the window," Serena said, pleased to see that her favorite spot in Lady Beatrice's drawing-room was vacant.

Without a word, the efficient maid who had finished making up their tray, carried it over and placed it on the low table before the couch that the ladies were making their way to.

"Thank you kindly." Serena smiled at the maid as she and Josephine took their seats.

Immediately, Josephine set about pouring them each some tea and then busied herself setting out the two plates and loading them with little sandwiches and cakes.

"The Wakefield Chase has always been important to my father. There is no prize, nor does he gain anything particular from it; it is more a matter of pride than anything else."

"The pride of competition?"

"Yes, but it is not always who wins or loses the Wakefield Chase itself, but rather who is better placed out of my family and the family of the Duke of Shawcross."

"Your father and the Duke of Shawcross have some little competition between them?" Josephine said, entirely interested.

Ordinarily, Serena did not particularly talk of the unspoken rivalry between her father and the Duke. Nor did she talk of the way that that rivalry had tumbled down the generations and firmly affixed itself to not only her, but also the Duke's son. However, Josephine really did seem so interested in Serena's world and she thought it would be churlish to simply give her the racing facts without any matters of human interest whatsoever. And had she not just promised Josephine that they would be themselves at all times?

"If I am entirely honest, Josephine, it is more of a rivalry than simple competition. My father and the Duke are not friends and never have been. We compete at many of the same equestrian events for several counties across, but it is the Wakefield Chase which has always seemed to be the race we must win."

"But do you know why? Do you know what it is about that

particular race that the two men find so important?" As Josephine nibbled her sandwich, she seemed entirely transfixed by the revelations.

"I have no idea. I suppose it is a thing which has been in place for so long that I have never questioned it. Even as a small child, I knew that the Wakefield Chase was of the utmost importance."

"You never asked your father why?"

"No, I suppose that seems silly, really." Serena spoke a little vaguely as she thought about it. She really had never asked him and, whilst she supposed it was because she had grown up with that particular knowledge, she also wondered if the truth was that she did not really dare ask him after so many years. "But I must say, it is easy to see why there is a certain rivalry between my father and the Duke of Shawcross. Whilst I do not know the Duke particularly well, I find that his son and I have a similar, quite unspoken rivalry between us."

"The Duke's son is Lord Elliot Beckett, is he not?" Josephine said, the dainty china teacup in her hand pausing mid-air.

"Yes." Serena nodded.

"But he is here today, is he not?"

"Yes, I do believe I have seen him. He is a regular visitor to Lady Wakefield and I suppose, barring equestrian events, this is where he and I cross paths the most."

"So, does the Wakefield Chase have something to do with Lady Wakefield?" Josephine reached for another sandwich. "You must forgive my ignorance in all of this, and my questions, but I find myself intrigued."

"I do not mind at all, Josephine. Most other ladies are not particularly interested to hear any of this and so I am very pleased to have someone with whom I can talk about my passions." Serena paused to take a sip of tea. "The Wakefield Chase is an event that was originally set up by Lady Beatrice's late husband, Lord Oscar Wakefield. It has been running these thirty years and I do believe the very first Wakefield Chase was in the early autumn of 1786."

"And when did your father and the Duke begin to compete in the thing?"

"Oh, they were at the very first race. Back then, they both rode their own horses, rather than have jockeys ride for them."

"So, it was a competition in every sense back then?"

"It most certainly was, but I was still a girl when it seemed they both decided to concentrate on the training of their horses and the taking on of skilled jockeys. Both estates have a vast number of horses in their collection now. Too many to ride personally."

"And I take it that you have a great interest in your father's horses? You have much to do with the running of things, such as interviewing jockeys and what have you?"

"Yes, I am afraid I am a terribly keen horsewoman, Josephine. I would give anything to take part in the Wakefield Chase myself," Serena whispered conspiratorially.

"I cannot help but think that you would certainly give the men of the county a run for their money," Josephine said, her eyes opening wide with some admiration. "I must admit, I am not terribly good with horses myself. I suppose it is because I did not spend a good deal of time with them when

I was growing up. My father had horses, of course, but the closest I usually got was on my way into the carriage. As a result, I find them a little unpredictable and just a little frightening."

"Well, you are not wrong, Josephine. Horses are somewhat unpredictable at times but it is simply a matter of getting to know them one by one. They all have their own different characteristics and habits, much like people. The longer you spend with them, the sooner you learn their characteristics, even the ones they do not particularly want you to know about." Serena laughed.

"And so, you spend a good deal of time with the horses?"

"Much of my day is spent around the stables. My mother has long since given up despairing of me and my urchin appearance as I go about my day-to-day business. But we do have a great number of horses and staff and riders to look after them. I do much of the overseeing so that I might help my father. My brother is but twelve-years-old and is not yet skilled enough to be able to help my father."

"I wonder if it has been of great benefit to you to have only a younger brother. After all, had you an older brother or one who was just a year or two beneath you, you might not have had so great an involvement in things."

"That is absolutely true," Serena said shaking her head thoughtfully. "I am almost ten years older than my brother and I think my father had begun to despair of producing an heir for his title of Earl. But I must admit, for my own purpose, it has given me a good deal of freedom to help and it has focused my father's attentions upon my own skills these last few years. Rupert really was too tiny."

"So, in the end, your father must be very pleased of your interest as he waits for his son to grow up."

"Yes, I do believe he is. It has become something quite natural to him to discuss the horses and the racing with me as an equal, and I quite naturally found out every detail of running the stables. And it is a thing I oversee currently even more than my father."

"How wonderful, truly. What a marvelous thing to have such an interest and a passion. I must admit myself a little envious."

"I daresay you have a great many things to occupy you, especially having all the duties of a Countess and an infant to tend to." Serena laughed.

"Yes, I suppose that does not leave a good deal of time for anything else." Josephine joined her in laughter. "But it is probably the same for your father. After all, he will have all of his duties and responsibilities as the Earl of Winfield, so you must be a good deal of use to him in overseeing his equestrian interests."

"Yes, indeed," Serena said and bit into a most delightful sandwich which was filled with some sort of fish mousse. "Josephine, have you tried one of these?" Serena asked with a look of purest pleasure on her face. "The fish mousse ones?"

"No, but I shall if they are that good," she said, reaching out herself.

As the two women ate in silence for a few moments, Serena thought of her father. It was true that he had not paid as much attention to the stables and the horses of late and she knew in her heart it was not entirely the duties and responsibilities of the Winfield Estate of which he was Earl.

After all, he had always employed an overseer and an estate manager to lessen the load.

Serena suddenly felt a little low as she thought of the curious mood her father had been in for more than a year now. He seemed to grow ever quieter and ever more distant and his face had taken on the countenance of a much older man. She knew that he must have some care or other eating away at him. A concern which seemed to take up a good deal of his time. And yet, just as in the matter of why he and the Duke of Shawcross were such rivals, Serena had found that she dared not ask.

Only once she had approached her mother, hoping for some indication, but there had just been disappointed. It seemed that her mother was either none the wiser, or she was keeping a secret of some sort. Either way, it had left Serena with a nagging feeling that all was not as it should be and she wished for all the world that she could get to the bottom of it.

"Serena, are you quite all right?" Josephine asked.

Serena looked up to find her new friend looking at her with some concern.

"Yes, thank you. I fear I have perhaps eaten one too many of these delightful little sandwiches." She shrugged and smiled.

"With little wonder." Josephine looked down at her plate. "They really are as delightful as you said they would be." Josephine reached for yet another and both women laughed.

Find out if Serena can win her race or if more is at stake in A Race Against the Duke.

LOVE AGAINST THE ODDS AN 11 BOOK REGENCY BOX SET PREVIEW

You will love the 11 romances in this wonderful value box set reduced to 0.99 for a short time only – also FREE on KU
http://amzn.to/2yaMoIg

* * *

"Perhaps we should write to Bridgette and tell her all about it." Freya said, her young face crinkled in an expression of the very deepest concern.

"But what will that achieve, Freya?" Cecilia asked, sitting down heavily amongst a rustle of taffeta upon the little stool at her dressing table as she sighed heavily.

"There might be something that she can do to help us. After all, her husband is a baron. Perhaps Lord William will be able to do something about it all." Freya began to sound a little panicked, almost as if she had begun to realize that there was very little either woman could do about the situation.

"I don't think so, Freya. Whilst it is true that Lord William is a baron, Hunter Rowley is the Earl of Aston. I really do not think that there is anything that William De Clare could do when faced with an Earl of the Realm."

"But is the Earl of Aston really so terrible?"

"I do not know if he is good or bad, Freya. And that is the thing that terrifies me. I know nothing about him whatsoever, and can find nothing much about his personality or standards from any one of our acquaintance."

"Except that he's scarred," Freya said, her eyebrows raising. "Many say that he is a beast… that no one will marry him even though he is an Earl!"

Cecilia raised her own eyebrows and saw the color hit her sister's cheeks. They did not judge people on their looks. "Yes, he's scarred, but that tells me nothing about the man he is, does it now? It doesn't tell me if he's cruel or kind, it simply tells me that he has suffered some kind of misfortune," Cecilia said, somewhat regretting the tone of frustration in her voice.

"Oh, I'm sorry, Cecilia," Freya said, genuinely apologetic.

"Oh, my dear sister! It is I who should be begging your forgiveness. None of this is your fault, and there is nothing that either of us can do about it. I am simply fearful of the situation itself, and I rather let my frustration fall upon you. Please forgive me." Cecilia was absolutely determined not to cry. For one thing, she did not yet know if tears were truly called for. After all, the Earl might not be so terribly disfigured, and he might yet prove to be a decent man. Furthermore, Cecilia was determined not to upset her younger sister with her tears. Freya was a sweet and loving girl, and if she thought Cecilia had been brought to the point of tears, she would never sleep for worry.

"Please, think nothing of it, Cecilia. You must be most dreadfully worried, as am I," Freya said, darting across the dimly lit bedroom to place her hands upon her sister's shoulders. "So you really think that Lord William would have no sway whatsoever with the Earl?"

"In truth, I think not."

"But maybe there is another way Lord William De Clare can help us," Freya said, her face suddenly brightening as she seized upon her next thought. "Perhaps he can shelter us? Perhaps Lord William will allow you and I to go and live at Lockridge House with Bridgette?"

"Oh, what a wonderful idea, Freya," Cecilia said sadly. "But I fear that we cannot ask that of him. In truth, his responsibility towards our family ended when Mama married again."

Cecilia reflected bitterly upon the very reasonable allowance Lord William De Clare had paid monthly to their mother, Penelope Hampton, from the moment he married Bridgette. It had been a more than generous settlement, and certainly enough to keep the family in the home and stave off the near poverty in which Cecilia's selfish, pleasure seeking father had left them. Quite rightly, the allowance had ceased upon Penelope Hampton's second marriage.

"Oh, I suppose not. I rather think I'm simply clutching at straws, anything that will help," Freya said, moving to kneel beside the stool Cecilia was sitting on, and gently placing her head on her sister's lap.

"Please don't upset yourself so, Freya. After all, everything might turn out for the best in the end. Just look at Bridgette…; she had to marry for anything other than love, and yet still she found it where she had never expected to." Cecilia gently stroked her sister's glossy hair.

"I could only say this to you, Cecilia, but I truly wish that Mama had never married again," Freya's voice was muffled.

"Oh, and how I wish it too. For he is such an obstinate man." Cecilia shook her head absentmindedly from side to side, picturing her new stepfather.

Percival Cunningham's pursuit of Penelope Hampton began almost as soon as Bridgette had become married to Lord William De Clare. Percival had no title of his own, but was rather drawn to such things, and Bridgette's marriage had seemed, in his eyes, to elevate the rest of her family.

Percival was himself very wealthy, having wisely invested inherited money to the extent where his fortunes were often discussed in whispered conversations about the County. Percival himself was much less modest, and was keen that everybody should be very sensible of the fact that he was, indeed, one of the wealthiest men for many a mile. Many found his immodest behavior rather contemptible, and yet all were somehow in awe of his ability to exponentially increase his wealth, year upon year.

One of those people in awe of his wealth was Mrs. Penelope Hampton. Even before her first husband had frittered away their fortune, blaming his own excesses on the lack of a son, the Hampton family had certainly known nothing of the sort of wealth Percival Cunningham could boast. When Penelope Hampton compared the allowance provided by Lord William De Clare with everything that Percival Cunningham could provide, there was seemingly little contest. Percival Cunningham had not found it necessary to pursue Penelope Hampton for very long before she agreed to become his wife.

"He really is, Cecilia. There is not one thing about his character which I find I like, and nothing about the man that I would trust," Freya said, sounding a little afraid.

"I'm in complete agreement, Freya. And yet we must find some way to assimilate our lives into his, and his into ours. Mama is married to him now, and there is nothing that you or I can do to change that fact. I think it falls upon us to make the very best of it and hope that our efforts shall be enough."

"But the only way we can do that, Cecilia, is to bend to his will in all things. We must marry whomever he chooses for us, without argument, and we must creep about our own home here as if we are unwelcome guests."

"I know, Freya. I wonder if that is, in part at least, his reason for searching for a husband for me."

"You mean because he does not want us here, he's choosing to marry us off?"

"As I say, I think that may be a part of it."

"And the other part, Cecilia?"

"Percival Cunningham strikes me as a title snob. He only deemed our family good enough after Bridgette had married a baron. Prior to that, I feel sure that he showed no interest whatsoever in Mama."

"And you think his marrying you off to an Earl rather feeds his hunger for the sort of title he will never have?" Freya said, raising her eyebrows with an air of incredulity.

"Yes, I really do believe that."

"But he is already related to this Earl, is he not?"

"Yes he is, Freya, albeit in a rather vague sort of away. Percival Cunningham is a very distant cousin of Hunter Rowley."

"But is a distant cousin really in any sort of position to offer up a bride for the Earl of Aston?" Freya said, once again a certain amount of hope appearing in her eyes. As she looked at her sister, Cecilia could see that Freya was seizing upon any way in which the whole thing could be turned on its head; could be made untrue.

"Well yes, because the relationship was made rather closer by the circumstances of the young Earl."

"You mean, because the Earl of Aston lost his family when he was just a child?"

"Yes, because the only person with some claim to be a relative who was able to bring the child up was none other than Percival Cunningham."

"So the Earl looks upon Percival Cunningham as some sort of father figure, does he not?" Freya said, the hope which had lit her eyes just moments before was finally extinguished.

"That is what Percival led me to believe." Cecilia said, remembering the entire exchange with an uncontrollable shudder. "When he told me the whole thing."

Cecilia drifted off, once again being irresistibly drawn to relive the awful conversation in which all had been made very clear to her.

"But darling, an Earl! Just think of it!" Cecilia's mother had said with a rather over exuberant enthusiasm. Penelope Cunningham seemed rather delighted by the whole thing.

"Mama, I am not the least bit interested in his status. Titles do not mean to me what they obviously mean to you." Cecilia had been furious at what she perceived as her mother's lack of support for her and her wishes.

"You will not speak to your mother in that fashion, Cecilia," Percival Cunningham said with the sort of authoritative tones which most certainly were at odds with his short and thin stature.

"I really do not see what this has to do with you, Mr. Cunningham. After all, you most certainly are not my father," Cecilia had said, her chin very much set and her head held high.

"Since I married your mother, and provide everything including the clothes you stand up in, then you shall afford me every respect that a father deserves. And in that, young lady, I include the fact that you must always do as I tell you." Percival smirked, clearly finding himself to have the upper hand and thoroughly enjoying it.

"But Mama!" Cecilia had turned to look at her mother, in the vain hope that she would do or say something to help her.

"Oh, my dear child, please do not be awkward," was all that Penelope Cunningham could offer her middle daughter.

"Mama, I am not being simply awkward for the sake of it. I have never met this Earl, and I have no wish to marry at the moment. Since, as your husband continually points out, he has an excess of money, then I can see no real reason for you to be in such a hurry to marry me off." Cecilia could feel a certain coldness developing within her as she looked upon her mother's face. Penelope had always been concerned about money, and many had been the time that Cecilia had pitied the woman her worries. And yet, despite all of that, Cecilia had never really expected her mother's head to be so turned by fortune. It simply wasn't enough for her mother to live in comfort, as Lord William De Clare's allowance had enabled her to do, but rather she wanted to live ostentatiously, enjoying every comfort and privilege that life with Percival Cunningham could offer her.

"Penelope, could you leave us please," Percival said in a quiet and somewhat menacing voice. Much to Cecilia's horror, her mother gave her a dry smile before turning to leave the room. Cecilia had never suspected that her mother could be so easily dismissed. Money really did change everything.

"You will marry the Earl of Aston," Percival said, quite simply.

"I will not," Cecilia replied, with a quiet determination.

"I fail to see how it is that you think you can disobey me." Percival was eyeing her with an unveiled dislike.

"I shall not stay here, Mr. Cunningham. Rather, I shall go away and stay with relatives," Cecilia said, almost without thinking. In truth, the only relative she had was her sister Bridgette.

"No, you shall not leave this place. You will do as I tell you, and you will marry the Earl of Aston."

"I will not," Cecilia repeated. In her mind she felt like stamping her foot and shaking her fist as a small child would but in her heart she felt cold, dark dread. Would this marriage truly happen?

"If you do not do as I tell you, it shall be very much the worse for you, your sister, and your dear mother," he added the last with a cruel twist of his ugly, thin-lipped mouth.

Cecilia had always thought Percival Cunningham to be a

truly repugnant human being. He was so short in stature that he was barely the same height as her own mother, and much shorter than she herself was. He was also as thin as a rake, with wiry and angular features, and unpleasantly long-fingered hands. His cheeks were somewhat sunken, and his small, close-set dark eyes and long nose rather gave him the appearance of a vulture. When together, Percival and Penelope Cunningham looked like the most unlikely couple. Penelope was truly beautiful, looking far younger than her years. It must surely have been as clear to everybody else as it was to Cecilia that Penelope had simply married Percival Cunningham for money, and nothing but money. In that moment, her disappointment in her own mother could not have been greater.

"What do you mean by that, Mr. Cunningham?" The hair on the back of Cecilia's neck had risen uncomfortably. There was something most sincere in his countenance, not to mention very, very threatening.

"If you do not do as I instruct you, I shall ruin the reputations of not only your mother, but of you and your younger sister also." His smirk was the cruelest she had ever seen.

"And how do you intend to do that, sir?" Cecilia said, quite unable to hide her true hatred for him.

"I shall make it very clear that you and your younger sister were not sired by Edgar Hampton, but rather by someone else altogether. Someone with whom your mother was having an affair."

"Mr. Cunningham! My mother has never had an affair!" Cecilia's face flushed a violent red, and she could feel her little hands balling into fists. Quite what she thought she would do with the fists, Cecilia had no idea.

"Oh, you ridiculous girl! You mother does not need to have actually had an affair for me to be able to ruin her. It strikes me, young lady, that you have absolutely no idea who you're dealing with." For a moment, Percival Cunningham stood almost ape-fashion, holding his arms slightly out at his sides, almost as if to give the impression that he was very much larger than he truly was.

"But you cannot do that!" Cecilia said, almost incredulous.

"Oh, I can manage just about anything I put my mind to."

"But you would be ruining your own wife."

"I care no more for your mother than she cares for me, my dear. I shall ruin her, keep her as my wife, and humiliate her with a succession of mistresses. And after her alleged behavior is known far and wide, there will be none in the County who would blame me for my actions." Percival began to laugh, and it was truly a hateful sound.

"Surely you would not." Cecilia's eyes were wide with astonishment and fear.

"Well, Cecilia, my dear, I daresay that the only way you can discover whether or not I am bluffing is to push me. Refuse to marry the Earl of Aston, and risk everything. For not only will your mother be disgraced, but you and Freya will be shunned by every decent man in the County. You shall both be stuck here with me for eternity, and I shall make your lives a seething pit of misery."

"But I could tell mother everything you have told me."

"If you wish, then do so. It is of little matter to me. Your mother is my wife, and there is nothing that she can do against me. It matters not if she knows my plan, or if she does not know it."

"Cecilia? Cecilia?" Freya's gentle little voice brought Cecilia out of her evil daydream. "What is the matter?" Freya continued.

"Oh nothing, my dear. Like you, I am simply wondering what move to make next. In truth, I think there is none to make."

"But there must be." In some ways, Cecilia envied Freya her optimism. Not knowing the entire contents of the conversation Cecilia had suffered with Percival, Freya was able to naïvely cling to her hope that there must be something that could be done. Cecilia had decided that she would not tell Freya of the truly appalling threat that Percival had made. There was little point in it, and it would serve no purpose other than to upset her sister even further than she already was.

Cecilia was determined never to tell her younger sister the truth of what had been said in that meeting. If she had to carry around the bile from that evil conversation the rest of her life, then that was exactly what she would do. She would shield her sister from this one horror.

Get all eleven romances in this wonderful value box set for just 0.99 for a limited time only – also FREE on KU http://amzn.to/2yaMoIg

MORE BOOKS BY CHARLOTTE DARCY

All FREE on Kindle Unlimited

Latest Box Set

The Duke, the Earl, and the Joker

Latest Books novel length:

The Earl & Mrs. Dalloway

The Duke's Return and the Lady's Rebuttal

A Race Against the Duke

* * *

The Shallow Waters of Romance FREE

Regency romantic dreams - novel length books

The Broken Duke – Mended by Love

The Bluestocking, the Earl, and the Author

The Earl's Bitter Secret

Box Sets

<u>Love Against the Odds</u> an 11 Book Regency Box Set http://amzn.to/2ozBJlq

Now get all **The Montcrieff Novella's** including an exclusive book in one 6 book collection FREE on Kindle Unlimited.

Get a FREE eBook and find out about Charlotte's new releases by joining her newsletter here. Your information will never be shared. http://eepurl.com/bSNOLP

ABOUT THE AUTHOR

I hope you enjoyed these books by Charlotte Darcy.

Charlotte is a hopeless romantic. She loves historical romance and the Regency era the most. She has been a writer for many years and can think of nothing better than seeing how her characters can find their happy ever after.

She lives in Derbyshire, England and when not writing you will find her walking the British countryside with her dog Poppy or visiting stately homes, such as Chatsworth House which is local to her.

You can contact Charlotte at CharlotteDarcy@cd2.com or via facebook at @CharlotteDarcyAuthor

Or join my exclusive newsletter for a free book and updates on new releases here.

* * *

This is the end of this book. I hope you enjoyed out time together and look forward to many more romantic adventures. You can contact me on facebook at https://www.facebook.com/CharlotteDarcyAuthor/

God bless,

Charlotte Darcy

Printed in Great Britain
by Amazon

37160572R00067